I0535236

A Little Book of Profitable Tales by Eugene Field

Eugene Field was born on 2nd September 1850 in St. Louis, Missouri. His mother died when he was six and his father when he was nineteen. His academic life was not taken seriously and he preferred the life of a prankster until, in 1875, he began work as a journalist for the St. Joseph Gazette in Saint Joseph, Missouri.

In his career as a journalist he soon found a niche that suited him. His articles were light, humorous and written in a personal gossipy style that endeared him to his readership. Some were soon being syndicated to other newspapers around the States. Field soon rose to city editor of the Gazette.

Field had first published poetry in 1879, when his poem 'Christmas Treasures' appeared. This was the beginning that would eventually number over a dozen volumes. As well as verse Field published an extensive range of short stories including 'The Holy Cross' and 'Daniel and the Devil.'

In 1889 whilst the family were in London and Field himself was recovering from a bout of ill health he wrote his most famous poem; 'Lovers Lane'.

On 4th November 1895 Eugene Field Sr died in Chicago of a heart attack at the age of 45.

Index of Contents

CHAPTER I

Once upon a time the forest was in a great commotion. Early in the evening the wise old cedars had shaken their heads ominously and predicted strange things. They had lived in the forest many, many years; but never had they seen such marvellous sights as were to be seen now in the sky, and upon the hills, and in the distant village.

"Pray tell us what you see," pleaded a little vine; "we who are not as tall as you can behold none of these wonderful things. Describe them to us, that we may enjoy them with you."

"I am filled with such amazement," said one of the cedars, "that I can hardly speak. The whole sky seems to be aflame, and the stars appear to be dancing among the clouds; angels walk down from heaven to the earth, and enter the village or talk with the shepherds upon the hills."

The vine listened in mute astonishment. Such things never before had happened. The vine trembled with excitement. Its nearest neighbor was a tiny tree, so small it scarcely ever was noticed; yet it was a very beautiful little tree, and the vines and ferns and mosses and other humble residents of the forest loved it dearly.

"How I should like to see the angels!" sighed the little tree, "and how I should like to see the stars dancing among the clouds! It must be very beautiful."

As the vine and the little tree talked of these things, the cedars watched with increasing interest the wonderful scenes over and beyond the confines of the forest. Presently they thought they heard music, and they were not mistaken, for soon the whole air was full of the sweetest harmonies ever heard upon earth.

"What beautiful music!" cried the little tree. "I wonder whence it comes."

"The angels are singing," said a cedar; "for none but angels could make such sweet music."

"But the stars are singing, too," said another cedar; "yes, and the shepherds on the hills join in the song, and what a strangely glorious song it is!"

The trees listened to the singing, but they did not understand its meaning: it seemed to be an anthem, and it was of a Child that had been born; but further than this they did not understand. The strange and glorious song continued all the night; and all that night the angels walked to and fro, and the shepherd-folk talked with the angels, and the stars danced and carolled in high heaven. And it was nearly morning when the cedars cried out, "They are coming to the forest! the angels are coming to the forest!" And, surely enough, this was true. The vine and the little tree were very terrified, and they begged their older and stronger neighbors to protect them from harm. But the cedars were too busy with their own fears to pay any heed to the faint pleadings of the humble vine and the little tree. The angels came into the forest, singing the same glorious anthem about the Child, and the stars sang in chorus with them, until every part of the woods rang with echoes of that wondrous song. There was nothing in the appearance of this angel host to inspire fear; they were clad all in white, and there were crowns upon their fair heads, and golden harps in their hands; love, hope, charity, compassion, and joy beamed from their beautiful faces, and their presence seemed to fill the forest with a divine peace. The angels came through the forest to where the little tree stood, and gathering around it, they touched it with their hands, and kissed its little branches, and sang even more sweetly than before. And their song was about the Child, the Child, the Child that had been born. Then the stars came down from the skies and danced and hung upon the branches of the tree, and they, too, sang that song,—the song of the Child. And all the other trees and the vines and the ferns and the mosses beheld in wonder; nor could they understand why all these things were being done, and why this exceeding honor should be shown the little tree.

When the morning came the angels left the forest,—all but one angel, who remained behind and lingered near the little tree. Then a cedar asked: "Why do you tarry with us, holy angel?" And the angel answered: "I stay to guard this little tree, for it is sacred, and no harm shall come to it."

The little tree felt quite relieved by this assurance, and it held up its head more confidently than ever before. And how it thrived and grew, and waxed in strength and beauty! The cedars said they never had seen the like. The sun seemed to lavish its choicest rays upon the little tree, heaven dropped its sweetest dew upon it, and the winds never came to the forest that they did not forget their rude manners and linger to kiss the little tree and sing it their prettiest songs. No danger ever menaced it, no harm threatened; for the angel never slept,—through the day and through the night the angel watched the little tree and protected it from all evil. Oftentimes the trees talked with the angel; but of course they understood little of what he said, for he spoke always of the Child who was to become the Master; and always when thus he talked, he caressed the little tree, and stroked its branches and leaves, and moistened them with his tears. It all was so very strange that none in the forest could understand.

So the years passed, the angel watching his blooming charge. Sometimes the beasts strayed toward the little tree and threatened to devour its tender foliage; sometimes the woodman came with his axe, intent upon hewing down the straight and comely thing; sometimes the hot, consuming breath of drought swept from the south, and sought to blight the forest and all its verdure: the angel kept them from the little tree. Serene and beautiful it grew, until now it was no longer a little tree, but the pride and glory of the forest.

One day the tree heard some one coming through the forest. Hitherto the angel had hastened to its side when men approached; but now the angel strode away and stood under the cedars yonder.

"Dear angel," cried the tree, "can you not hear the footsteps of some one approaching? Why do you leave me?"

"Have no fear," said the angel; "for He who comes is the Master."

The Master came to the tree and beheld it. He placed His hands upon its smooth trunk and branches, and the tree was thrilled with a strange and glorious delight. Then He stooped and kissed the tree, and then He turned and went away.

Many times after that the Master came to the forest, and when He came it always was to where the tree stood. Many times He rested beneath the tree and enjoyed the shade of its foliage, and listened to the music of the wind as it swept through the rustling leaves. Many times He slept there, and the tree watched over Him, and the forest was still, and all its voices were hushed. And the angel hovered near like a faithful sentinel.

Ever and anon men came with the Master to the forest, and sat with Him in the shade of the tree, and talked with Him of matters which the tree never could understand; only it heard that the talk was of love and charity and gentleness, and it saw that the Master was beloved and venerated by the others. It heard them tell of the Master's goodness and humility,—how He had healed the sick and raised the dead and bestowed inestimable blessings wherever He walked. And the tree loved the Master for His beauty and His goodness; and when He came to the forest it was full of joy, but when He came not it was sad. And the other trees of the forest joined in its happiness and its sorrow, for they, too, loved the Master. And the angel always hovered near.

The Master came one night alone into the forest, and His face was pale with anguish and wet with tears, and He fell upon His knees and prayed. The tree heard Him, and all the forest was still, as if it were standing in the presence of death. And when the morning came, lo! the angel had gone.

Then there was a great confusion in the forest. There was a sound of rude voices, and a clashing of swords and staves. Strange men appeared, uttering loud oaths and cruel threats, and the tree was filled with terror. It called aloud for the angel, but the angel came not.

"Alas," cried the vine, "they have come to destroy the tree, the pride and glory of the forest!"

The forest was sorely agitated, but it was in vain. The strange men plied their axes with cruel vigor, and the tree was hewn to the ground. Its beautiful branches were cut away and cast aside, and its soft, thick foliage was strewn to the tenderer mercies of the winds.

"They are killing me!" cried the tree; "why is not the angel here to protect me?"

But no one heard the piteous cry,—none but the other trees of the forest; and they wept, and the little vine wept too.

Then the cruel men dragged the despoiled and hewn tree from the forest, and the forest saw that beauteous thing no more.

But the night wind that swept down from the City of the Great King that night to ruffle the bosom of distant Galilee, tarried in the forest awhile to say that it had seen that day a cross upraised on Calvary,—the tree on which was stretched the body of the dying Master.

CHAPTER II

THE SYMBOL AND THE SAINT

Once upon a time a young man made ready for a voyage. His name was Norss; broad were his shoulders, his cheeks were ruddy, his hair was fair and long, his body betokened strength, and good-nature shone from his blue eyes and lurked about the corners of his mouth.

"Where are you going?" asked his neighbor Jans, the forge-master.

"I am going sailing for a wife," said Norss.

"For a wife, indeed!" cried Jans. "And why go you to seek her in foreign lands? Are not our maidens good enough and fair enough, that you must need search for a wife elsewhere? For shame, Norss! for shame!"

But Norss said, "A spirit came to me in my dreams last night and said, 'Launch the boat and set sail to-morrow. Have no fear; for I will guide you to the bride that awaits you.' Then, standing there, all white and beautiful, the spirit held forth a symbol—such as I had never before seen—in the figure of a cross, and the spirit said: 'By this symbol shall she be known to you.'"

"If this be so, you must need go," said Jans. "But are you well victualled? Come to my cabin, and let me give you venison and bear's meat."

Norss shook his head. "The spirit will provide," said he. "I have no fear, and I shall take no care, trusting in the spirit."

So Norss pushed his boat down the beach into the sea, and leaped into the boat, and unfurled the sail to the wind. Jans stood wondering on the beach, and watched the boat speed out of sight.

On, on, many days on sailed Norss,—so many leagues that he thought he must have compassed the earth. In all this time he knew no hunger nor thirst; it was as the spirit had told him in his dream,— no cares nor dangers beset him. By day the dolphins and the other creatures of the sea gambolled about his boat; by night a beauteous Star seemed to direct his course; and when he slept and dreamed, he saw ever the spirit clad in white, and holding forth to him the symbol in the similitude of a cross.

At last he came to a strange country,—a country so very different from his own that he could scarcely trust his senses. Instead of the rugged mountains of the North, he saw a gentle landscape of velvety green; the trees were not pines and firs, but cypresses, cedars, and palms; instead of the cold, crisp air of his native land, he scented the perfumed zephyrs of the Orient; and the wind that filled the sail of his boat and smote his tanned cheeks was heavy and hot with the odor of cinnamon and spices. The waters were calm and blue,—very different from the white and angry waves of Norss's native fiord.

As if guided by an unseen hand, the boat pointed straight for the beach of this strangely beautiful land; and ere its prow cleaved the shallower waters, Norss saw a maiden standing on the shore, shading her eyes with her right hand, and gazing intently at him. She was the most beautiful maiden he had ever looked upon. As Norss was fair, so was this maiden dark; her black hair fell loosely about her shoulders in charming contrast with the white raiment in which her slender, graceful form was clad. Around her neck she wore a golden chain, and therefrom was suspended a small symbol, which Norss did not immediately recognize.

"Hast thou come sailing out of the North into the East?" asked the maiden.

"Yes," said Norss.

"And thou art Norss?" she asked.

"I am Norss; and I come seeking my bride," he answered.

"I am she," said the maiden. "My name is Faia. An angel came to me in my dreams last night, and the angel said: 'Stand upon the beach to-day, and Norss shall come out of the North to bear thee home a bride.' So, coming here, I found thee sailing to our shore."

Remembering then the spirit's words, Norss said: "What symbol have you, Faia, that I may know how truly you have spoken?"

"No symbol have I but this," said Faia, holding out the symbol that was attached to the golden chain about her neck. Norss looked upon it, and lo! it was the symbol of his dreams,—a tiny wooden cross.

Then Norss clasped Faia in his arms and kissed her, and entering into the boat they sailed away into the North. In all their voyage neither care nor danger beset them; for as it had been told to them in their dreams, so it came to pass. By day the dolphins and the other creatures of the sea gambolled about them; by night the winds and the waves sang them to sleep; and, strangely enough, the Star which before had led Norss into the East, now shone bright and beautiful in the Northern sky!

When Norss and his bride reached their home, Jans, the forge-master, and the other neighbors made great joy, and all said that Faia was more beautiful than any other maiden in the land. So merry was Jans that he built a huge fire in his forge, and the flames thereof filled the whole Northern sky with rays of light that danced up, up, up to the Star, singing glad songs the while. So Norss and Faia were wed, and they went to live in the cabin in the fir-grove.

To these two was born in good time a son, whom they named Claus. On the night that he was born wondrous things came to pass. To the cabin in the fir-grove came all the quaint, weird spirits,—the fairies, the elves, the trolls, the pixies, the fadas, the crions, the goblins, the kobolds, the moss-people, the gnomes, the dwarfs, the water-sprites, the courils, the bogles, the brownies, the nixies, the trows, the stille-volk,—all came to the cabin in the fir-grove, and capered about and sang the strange, beautiful songs of the Mist-Land. And the flames of old Jans's forge leaped up higher than ever into the Northern sky, carrying the joyous tidings to the Star, and full of music was that happy night.

Even in infancy Claus did marvellous things. With his baby hands he wrought into pretty figures the willows that were given him to play with. As he grew older, he fashioned, with the knife old Jans had made for him, many curious toys,—carts, horses, dogs, lambs, houses, trees, cats, and birds, all of wood and very like to nature. His mother taught him how to make dolls too,—dolls of every kind, condition, temper, and color; proud dolls, homely dolls, boy dolls, lady dolls, wax dolls, rubber dolls, paper dolls, worsted dolls, rag dolls,—dolls of every description and without end. So Claus became at once quite as popular with the little girls as with the little boys of his native village; for he was so generous that he gave away all these pretty things as fast as he made them.

Claus seemed to know by instinct every language. As he grew older he would ramble off into the woods and talk with the trees, the rocks, and the beasts of the greenwood; or he would sit on the cliffs overlooking the fiord, and listen to the stories that the waves of the sea loved to tell him; then, too, he knew the haunts of the elves and the stille-volk, and many a pretty tale he learned from these little people. When night came, old Jans told him the quaint legends of the North, and his mother sang to him the lullabies she had heard when a little child herself in the far-distant East. And every night his mother held out to him the symbol in the similitude of the cross, and bade him kiss it ere he went to sleep.

So Claus grew to manhood, increasing each day in knowledge and in wisdom. His works increased too; and his liberality dispensed everywhere the beauteous things which his fancy conceived and his skill executed. Jans, being now a very old man, and having no son of his own, gave to Claus his forge and workshop, and taught him those secret arts which he in youth had learned from cunning masters. Right joyous now was Claus; and many, many times the Northern sky glowed with the flames that danced singing from the forge while Claus moulded his pretty toys. Every color of the rainbow were these flames; for they reflected the bright colors of the beauteous things strewn round that wonderful workshop. Just as of old he had dispensed to all children alike the homelier toys of his youth, so now he gave to all children alike these more beautiful and more curious gifts. So little children everywhere loved Claus, because he gave them pretty toys, and their parents loved him because he made their little ones so happy.

But now Norss and Faia were come to old age. After long years of love and happiness, they knew that death could not be far distant. And one day Faia said to Norss: "Neither you nor I, dear love, fear death; but if we could choose, would we not choose to live always in this our son Claus, who has been so sweet a joy to us?"

"Ay, ay," said Norss; "but how is that possible?"

"We shall see," said Faia.

That night Norss dreamed that a spirit came to him, and that the spirit said to him: "Norss, thou shalt surely live forever in thy son Claus, if thou wilt but acknowledge the symbol."

Then when the morning was come Norss told his dream to Faia, his wife; and Faia said,—

"The same dream had I,—an angel appearing to me and speaking these very words."

"But what of the symbol?" cried Norss.

"I have it here, about my neck," said Faia.

So saying, Faia drew from her bosom the symbol of wood,—a tiny cross suspended about her neck by the golden chain. And as she stood there holding the symbol out to Norss, he—he thought of the time when first he saw her on the far-distant Orient shore, standing beneath the Star in all her maidenly glory, shading her beauteous eyes with one hand, and with the other clasping the cross,— the holy talisman of her faith.

"Faia, Faia!" cried Norss, "it is the same,—the same you wore when I fetched you a bride from the East!"

"It is the same," said Faia, "yet see how my kisses and my prayers have worn it away; for many, many times in these years, dear Norss, have I pressed it to my lips and breathed your name upon it. See now—see what a beauteous light its shadow makes upon your aged face!"

The sunbeams, indeed, streaming through the window at that moment, cast the shadow of the symbol on old Norss's brow. Norss felt a glorious warmth suffuse him, his heart leaped with joy, and he stretched out his arms and fell about Faia's neck, and kissed the symbol and acknowledged it. Then likewise did Faia; and suddenly the place was filled with a wondrous brightness and with strange music, and never thereafter were Norss and Faia beholden of men.

Until late that night Claus toiled at his forge; for it was a busy season with him, and he had many, many curious and beauteous things to make for the little children in the country round about. The colored flames leaped singing from his forge, so that the Northern sky seemed to be lighted by a thousand rainbows; but above all this voiceful glory beamed the Star, bright, beautiful, serene.

Coming late to the cabin in the fir-grove, Claus wondered that no sign of his father or of his mother was to be seen. "Father—mother!" he cried, but he received no answer. Just then the Star cast its golden gleam through the latticed window, and this strange, holy light fell and rested upon the symbol of the cross that lay upon the floor. Seeing it, Claus stooped and picked it up, and kissing it reverently, he cried: "Dear talisman, be thou my inspiration evermore; and wheresoever thy blessed influence is felt, there also let my works be known henceforth forever!"

No sooner had he said these words than Claus felt the gift of immortality bestowed upon him; and in that moment, too, there came to him a knowledge that his parents' prayer had been answered, and that Norss and Faia would live in him through all time.

And lo! to that place and in that hour came all the people of Mist-Land and of Dream-Land to declare allegiance to him: yes, the elves, the fairies, the pixies,—all came to Claus, prepared to do his bidding. Joyously they capered about him, and merrily they sang.

"Now haste ye all," cried Claus,—"haste ye all to your homes and bring to my workshop the best ye have. Search, little hill-people, deep in the bowels of the earth for finest gold and choicest jewels; fetch me, O mermaids, from the bottom of the sea the treasures hidden there,—the shells of rainbow tints, the smooth, bright pebbles, and the strange ocean flowers; go, pixies, and other water-sprites, to your secret lakes, and bring me pearls! Speed! speed you all! for many pretty things have we to make for the little ones of earth we love!"

But to the kobolds and the brownies Claus said: "Fly to every house on earth where the cross is known; loiter unseen in the corners, and watch and hear the children through the day. Keep a strict account of good and bad, and every night bring back to me the names of good and bad, that I may know them."

The kobolds and the brownies laughed gleefully, and sped away on noiseless wings; and so, too, did the other fairies and elves.

There came also to Claus the beasts of the forest and the birds of the air, and bade him be their master. And up danced the Four Winds, and they said: "May we not serve you, too?"

The Snow King came stealing along in his feathery chariot. "Oho!" he cried, "I shall speed over all the world and tell them you are coming. In town and country, on the mountain-tops and in the valleys,— wheresoever the cross is raised,—there will I herald your approach, and thither will I strew you a pathway of feathery white. Oho! oho!" So, singing softly, the Snow King stole upon his way.

But of all the beasts that begged to do him service, Claus liked the reindeer best. "You shall go with me in my travels; for henceforth I shall bear my treasures not only to the children of the North, but to the children in every land whither the Star points me and where the cross is lifted up!" So said Claus to the reindeer, and the reindeer neighed joyously and stamped their hoofs impatiently, as though they longed to start immediately.

Oh, many, many times has Claus whirled away from his far Northern home in his sledge drawn by the reindeer, and thousands upon thousands of beautiful gifts—all of his own making—has he borne to the children of every land; for he loves them all alike, and they all alike love him, I trow. So truly do they love him that they call him Santa Claus, and I am sure that he must be a saint; for he has lived these many hundred years, and we, who know that he was born of Faith and Love, believe that he will live forever.

CHAPTER III

THE COMING OF THE PRINCE

I

"Whirr-r-r! whirr-r-r! whirr-r-r!" said the wind, and it tore through the streets of the city that Christmas eve, turning umbrellas inside out, driving the snow in fitful gusts before it, creaking the rusty signs and shutters, and playing every kind of rude prank it could think of.

"How cold your breath is to-night!" said Barbara, with a shiver, as she drew her tattered little shawl the closer around her benumbed body.

"Whirr-r-r! whirr-r-r! whirr-r-r!" answered the wind; "but why are you out in this storm? You should be at home by the warm fire."

"I have no home," said Barbara; and then she sighed bitterly, and something like a tiny pearl came in the corner of one of her sad blue eyes.

But the wind did not hear her answer, for it had hurried up the street to throw a handful of snow in the face of an old man who was struggling along with a huge basket of good things on each arm.

"Why are you not at the cathedral?" asked a snowflake, as it alighted on Barbara's shoulder. "I heard grand music, and saw beautiful lights there as I floated down from the sky a moment ago."

"What are they doing at the cathedral?" inquired Barbara.

"Why, haven't you heard?" exclaimed the snowflake. "I supposed everybody knew that the prince was coming to-morrow."

"Surely enough; this is Christmas eve," said Barbara, "and the prince will come to-morrow."

Barbara remembered that her mother had told her about the prince, how beautiful and good and kind and gentle he was, and how he loved the little children; but her mother was dead now, and there was none to tell Barbara of the prince and his coming,—none but the little snowflake.

"I should like to see the prince," said Barbara, "for I have heard he was very beautiful and good."

"That he is," said the snowflake. "I have never seen him, but I heard the pines and the firs singing about him as I floated over the forest to-night."

"Whirr-r-r! whirr-r-r!" cried the wind, returning boisterously to where Barbara stood. "I've been looking for you everywhere, little snowflake! So come with me."

And without any further ado, the wind seized upon the snowflake and hurried it along the street and led it a merry dance through the icy air of the winter night.

Barbara trudged on through the snow and looked in at the bright things in the shop windows. The glitter of the lights and the sparkle of the vast array of beautiful Christmas toys quite dazzled her. A strange mingling of admiration, regret, and envy filled the poor little creature's heart.

"Much as I may yearn to have them, it cannot be," she said to herself, "yet I may feast my eyes upon them."

"Go away from here!" said a harsh voice.

"How can the rich people see all my fine things if you stand before the window? Be off with you, you miserable little beggar!"

It was the shop-keeper, and he gave Barbara a savage box on the ear that sent her reeling into the deeper snowdrifts of the gutter.

Presently she came to a large house where there seemed to be much mirth and festivity. The shutters were thrown open, and through the windows Barbara could see a beautiful Christmas tree in the centre of a spacious room,—a beautiful Christmas tree ablaze with red and green lights, and heavy with toys and stars and glass balls, and other beautiful things that children love. There was a merry throng around the tree, and the children were smiling and gleeful, and all in that house seemed content and happy. Barbara heard them singing, and their song was about the prince who was to come on the morrow.

"This must be the house where the prince will stop," thought Barbara. "How I would like to see his face and hear his voice!—yet what would he care for me, a 'miserable little beggar'?"

So Barbara crept on through the storm, shivering and disconsolate, yet thinking of the prince.

"Where are you going?" she asked of the wind as it overtook her.

"To the cathedral," laughed the wind. "The great people are flocking there, and I will have a merry time amongst them, ha, ha, ha!"

And with laughter the wind whirled away and chased the snow toward the cathedral.

"It is there, then, that the prince will come," thought Barbara. "It is a beautiful place, and the people will pay him homage there. Perhaps I shall see him if I go there."

So she went to the cathedral. Many folk were there in their richest apparel, and the organ rolled out its grand music, and the people sang wondrous songs, and the priests made eloquent prayers; and the music, and the songs, and the prayers were all about the prince and his expected coming. The throng that swept in and out of the great edifice talked always of the prince, the prince, the prince, until Barbara really loved him very much, for all the gentle words she heard the people say of him.

"Please, can I go and sit inside?" inquired Barbara of the sexton.

"No!" said the sexton, gruffly, for this was an important occasion with the sexton, and he had no idea of wasting words on a beggar child.

"But I will be very good and quiet," pleaded Barbara. "Please may I not see the prince?"

"I have said no, and I mean it," retorted the sexton. "What have you for the prince, or what cares the prince for you? Out with you, and don't be blocking up the doorway!" So the sexton gave Barbara an angry push, and the child fell half-way down the icy steps of the cathedral. She began to cry. Some great people were entering the cathedral at the time, and they laughed to see her falling.

"Have you seen the prince?" inquired a snowflake, alighting on Barbara's cheek. It was the same little snowflake that had clung to her shawl an hour ago, when the wind came galloping along on his boisterous search.

"Ah, no!" sighed Barbara, in tears; "but what cares the prince for me?"

"Do not speak so bitterly," said the little snowflake. "Go to the forest and you shall see him, for the prince always comes through the forest to the city."

Despite the cold, and her bruises, and her tears, Barbara smiled. In the forest she could behold the prince coming on his way; and he would not see her, for she would hide among the trees and vines.

"Whirr-r-r, whirr-r-r!" It was the mischievous, romping wind once more; and it fluttered Barbara's tattered shawl, and set her hair to streaming in every direction, and swept the snowflake from her cheek and sent it spinning through the air.

Barbara trudged toward the forest. When she came to the city gate the watchman stopped her, and held his big lantern in her face, and asked her who she was and where she was going.

"I am Barbara, and I am going into the forest," said she, boldly.

"Into the forest?" cried the watchman, "and in this storm? No, child; you will perish!"

"But I am going to see the prince," said Barbara. "They will not let me watch for him in the church, nor in any of their pleasant homes, so I am going into the forest."

The watchman smiled sadly. He was a kindly man; he thought of his own little girl at home.

"No, you must not go to the forest," said he, "for you would perish with the cold."

But Barbara would not stay. She avoided the watchman's grasp and ran as fast as ever she could through the city gate.

"Come back, come back!" cried the watchman; "you will perish in the forest!"

But Barbara would not heed his cry. The falling snow did not stay her, nor did the cutting blast. She thought only of the prince, and she ran straightway to the forest.

II

"What do you see up there, O pine-tree?" asked a little vine in the forest. "You lift your head among the clouds to-night, and you tremble strangely as if you saw wondrous sights."

"I see only the distant hill-tops and the dark clouds," answered the pine-tree. "And the wind sings of the snow-king to-night; to all my questionings he says, 'Snow, snow, snow,' till I am wearied with his refrain."

"But the prince will surely come to-morrow?" inquired the tiny snowdrop that nestled close to the vine.

"Oh, yes," said the vine. "I heard the country folks talking about it as they went through the forest to-day, and they said that the prince would surely come on the morrow."

"What are you little folks down there talking about?" asked the pine-tree.

"We are talking about the prince," said the vine.

"Yes, he is to come on the morrow," said the pine-tree, "but not until the day dawns, and it is still all dark in the east."

"Yes," said the fir-tree, "the east is black, and only the wind and the snow issue from it."

"Keep your head out of my way!" cried the pine-tree to the fir; "with your constant bobbing around I can hardly see at all."

"Take that for your bad manners," retorted the fir, slapping the pine-tree savagely with one of her longest branches.

The pine-tree would put up with no such treatment, so he hurled his largest cone at the fir; and for a moment or two it looked as if there were going to be a serious commotion in the forest.

"Hush!" cried the vine in a startled tone; "there is some one coming through the forest."

The pine-tree and the fir stopped quarrelling, and the snowdrop nestled closer to the vine, while the vine hugged the pine-tree very tightly. All were greatly alarmed.

"Nonsense!" said the pine-tree, in a tone of assumed bravery. "No one would venture into the forest at such an hour."

"Indeed! and why not?" cried a child's voice. "Will you not let me watch with you for the coming of the prince?"

"Will you not chop me down?" inquired the pine-tree, gruffly.

"Will you not tear me from my tree?" asked the vine.

"Will you not pluck my blossoms?" plaintively piped the snowdrop.

"No, of course not," said Barbara; "I have come only to watch with you for the prince."

Then Barbara told them who she was, and how cruelly she had been treated in the city, and how she longed to see the prince, who was to come on the morrow. And as she talked, the forest and all therein felt a great compassion for her.

"Lie at my feet," said the pine-tree, "and I will protect you."

"Nestle close to me, and I will chafe your temples and body and limbs till they are warm," said the vine.

"Let me rest upon your cheek, and I will sing you my little songs," said the snowdrop.

And Barbara felt very grateful for all these homely kindnesses. She rested in the velvety snow at the foot of the pine-tree, and the vine chafed her body and limbs, and the little flower sang sweet songs to her.

"Whirr-r-r, whirr-r-r!" There was that noisy wind again, but this time it was gentler than it had been in the city.

"Here you are, my little Barbara," said the wind, in kindly tones. "I have brought you the little snowflake. I am glad you came away from the city, for the people are proud and haughty there; oh, but I will have my fun with them!"

Then, having dropped the little snowflake on Barbara's cheek, the wind whisked off to the city again. And we can imagine that it played rare pranks with the proud, haughty folk on its return; for the wind, as you know, is no respecter of persons.

"Dear Barbara," said the snowflake, "I will watch with thee for the coming of the prince."

And Barbara was glad, for she loved the little snowflake, that was so pure and innocent and gentle.

"Tell us, O pine-tree," cried the vine, "what do you see in the east? Has the prince yet entered the forest?"

"The east is full of black clouds," said the pine-tree, "and the winds that hurry to the hill-tops sing of the snow."

"But the city is full of brightness," said the fir. "I can see the lights in the cathedral, and I can hear wondrous music about the prince and his coming."

"Yes, they are singing of the prince in the cathedral," said Barbara, sadly.

"But we shall see him first," whispered the vine, reassuringly.

"Yes, the prince will come through the forest," said the little snowdrop, gleefully.

"Fear not, dear Barbara, we shall behold the prince in all his glory," cried the snowflake.

Then all at once there was a strange hubbub in the forest; for it was midnight, and the spirits came from their hiding-places to prowl about and to disport themselves. Barbara beheld them all in great wonder and trepidation, for she had never before seen the spirits of the forest, although she had often heard of them. It was a marvellous sight.

"Fear nothing," whispered the vine to Barbara,—"fear nothing, for they dare not touch you."

The antics of the wood-spirits continued but an hour; for then a cock crowed, and immediately thereat, with a wondrous scurrying, the elves and the gnomes and the other grotesque spirits sought their abiding places in the caves and in the hollow trunks and under the loose bark of the trees. And then it was very quiet once more in the forest.

"It is very cold," said Barbara. "My hands and feet are like ice."

Then the pine-tree and the fir shook down the snow from their broad boughs, and the snow fell upon Barbara and covered her like a white mantle.

"You will be warm now," said the vine, kissing Barbara's forehead. And Barbara smiled.

Then the snowdrop sang a lullaby about the moss that loved the violet. And Barbara said, "I am going to sleep; will you wake me when the prince comes through the forest?"

And they said they would. So Barbara fell asleep.

III

"The bells in the city are ringing merrily," said the fir, "and the music in the cathedral is louder and more beautiful than before. Can it be that the prince has already come into the city?"

"No," cried the pine-tree, "look to the east and see the Christmas day a-dawning! The prince is coming, and his pathway is through the forest!"

The storm had ceased. Snow lay upon all the earth. The hills, the forest, the city, and the meadows were white with the robe the storm-king had thrown over them. Content with his wondrous work, the storm-king himself had fled to his far Northern home before the dawn of the Christmas day. Everything was bright and sparkling and beautiful. And most beautiful was the great hymn of praise the forest sang that Christmas morning,—the pine-trees and the firs and the vines and the snow-flowers that sang of the prince and of his promised coming.

"Wake up, little one," cried the vine, "for the prince is coming!"

But Barbara slept; she did not hear the vine's soft calling, nor the lofty music of the forest.

A little snow-bird flew down from the fir-tree's bough and perched upon the vine, and carolled in Barbara's ear of the Christmas morning and of the coming of the prince. But Barbara slept; she did not hear the carol of the bird.

"Alas!" sighed the vine, "Barbara will not awaken, and the prince is coming."

Then the vine and the snowdrop wept, and the pine-tree and the fir were very sad.

The prince came through the forest clad in royal raiment and wearing a golden crown. Angels came with him, and the forest sang a great hymn unto the prince, such a hymn as had never before been heard on earth. The prince came to the sleeping child and smiled upon her and called her by name.

"Barbara, my little one," said the prince, "awaken, and come with me."

Then Barbara opened her eyes and beheld the prince. And it seemed as if a new life had come to her, for there was warmth in her body, and a flush upon her cheeks and a light in her eyes that were divine. And she was clothed no longer in rags, but in white flowing raiment; and upon the soft brown hair there was a crown like those which angels wear. And as Barbara arose and went to the prince, the little snowflake fell from her cheek upon her bosom, and forthwith became a pearl more precious than all other jewels upon earth.

And the prince took Barbara in his arms and blessed her, and turning round about, returned with the little child unto his home, while the forest and the sky and the angels sang a wondrous song.

The city waited for the prince, but he did not come. None knew of the glory of the forest that Christmas morning, nor of the new life that came to little Barbara.

Come thou, dear Prince, oh, come to us this holy Christmas time! Come to the busy marts of earth, the quiet homes, the noisy streets, the humble lanes; come to us all, and with thy love touch every human heart, that we may know that love, and in its blessed peace bear charity to all mankind!

CHAPTER IV

THE MOUSE AND THE MOONBEAM

Whilst you were sleeping, little Dear-my-Soul, strange things happened; but that I saw and heard them, I should never have believed them. The clock stood, of course, in the corner, a moonbeam floated idly on the floor, and a little mauve mouse came from the hole in the chimney corner and frisked and scampered in the light of the moonbeam upon the floor. The little mauve mouse was particularly merry; sometimes she danced upon two legs and sometimes upon four legs, but always very daintily and always very merrily.

"Ah, me!" sighed the old clock, "how different mice are nowadays from the mice we used to have in the good old times! Now there was your grandma, Mistress Velvetpaw, and there was your grandpa, Master Sniffwhisker,—how grave and dignified they were! Many a night have I seen them dancing upon the carpet below me, but always the stately minuet and never that crazy frisking which you are executing now, to my surprise—yes, and to my horror, too."

"But why shouldn't I be merry?" asked the little mauve mouse. "To-morrow is Christmas, and this is Christmas eve."

"So it is," said the old clock. "I had really forgotten all about it. But, tell me, what is Christmas to you, little Miss Mauve Mouse?"

"A great deal to me!" cried the little mauve mouse. "I have been very good a very long time: I have not used any bad words, nor have I gnawed any holes, nor have I stolen any canary seed, nor have I worried my mother by running behind the flour-barrel where that horrid trap is set. In fact, I have been so good that I'm very sure Santa Claus will bring me something very pretty."

This seemed to amuse the old clock mightily; in fact, the old clock fell to laughing so heartily that in an unguarded moment she struck twelve instead of ten, which was exceedingly careless and therefore to be reprehended.

"Why, you silly little mauve mouse," said the old clock, "you don't believe in Santa Claus, do you?"

"Of course I do," answered the little mauve mouse. "Believe in Santa Claus? Why shouldn't I? Didn't Santa Claus bring me a beautiful butter-cracker last Christmas, and a lovely gingersnap, and a delicious rind of cheese, and—and—lots of things? I should be very ungrateful if I did not believe in Santa Claus, and I certainly shall not disbelieve in him at the very moment when I am expecting him to arrive with a bundle of goodies for me.

"I once had a little sister," continued the little mauve mouse, "who did not believe in Santa Claus, and the very thought of the fate that befell her makes my blood run cold and my whiskers stand on end. She died before I was born, but my mother has told me all about her. Perhaps you never saw her; her name was Squeaknibble, and she was in stature one of those long, low, rangey mice that are seldom found in well-stocked pantries. Mother says that Squeaknibble took after our ancestors who came from New England, where the malignant ingenuity of the people and the ferocity of the cats rendered life precarious indeed. Squeaknibble seemed to inherit many ancestral traits, the most conspicuous of which was a disposition to sneer at some of the most respected dogmas in mousedom. From her very infancy she doubted, for example, the widely accepted theory that the moon was composed of green cheese; and this heresy was the first intimation her parents had of the sceptical turn of her mind. Of course, her parents were vastly annoyed, for their maturer natures saw that this youthful scepticism portended serious, if not fatal, consequences. Yet all in vain did the sagacious couple reason and plead with their headstrong and heretical child.

"For a long time Squeaknibble would not believe that there was any such archfiend as a cat; but she came to be convinced to the contrary one memorable night, on which occasion she lost two inches of her beautiful tail, and received so terrible a fright that for fully an hour afterward her little heart beat so violently as to lift her off her feet and bump her head against the top of our domestic hole. The cat that deprived my sister of so large a percentage of her vertebral colophon was the same brindled ogress that nowadays steals ever and anon into this room, crouches treacherously behind the sofa, and feigns to be asleep, hoping, forsooth, that some of us, heedless of her hated presence, will venture within reach of her diabolical claws. So enraged was this ferocious monster at the escape of my sister that she ground her fangs viciously together, and vowed to take no pleasure in life until she held in her devouring jaws the innocent little mouse which belonged to the mangled bit of tail she even then clutched in her remorseless claws."

"Yes," said the old clock, "now that you recall the incident, I recollect it well. I was here then, in this very corner, and I remember that I laughed at the cat and chided her for her awkwardness. My reproaches irritated her; she told me that a clock's duty was to run itself down, not to be depreciating the merits of others! Yes, I recall the time; that cat's tongue is fully as sharp as her claws."

"Be that as it may," said the little mauve mouse, "it is a matter of history, and therefore beyond dispute, that from that very moment the cat pined for Squeaknibble's life; it seemed as if that one little two-inch taste of Squeaknibble's tail had filled the cat with a consuming passion, or appetite, for the rest of Squeaknibble. So the cat waited and watched and hunted and schemed and devised and did everything possible for a cat—a cruel cat—to do in order to gain her murderous ends. One night—one fatal Christmas eve—our mother had undressed the children for bed, and was urging upon them to go to sleep earlier than usual, since she fully expected that Santa Claus would bring each of them something very palatable and nice before morning. Thereupon the little dears whisked their cunning tails, pricked up their beautiful ears, and began telling one another what they hoped Santa Claus would bring. One asked for a slice of Roquefort, another for Neufchatel, another for Sap Sago, and a fourth for Edam; one expressed a preference for de Brie, while another hoped to get Parmesan; one clamored for imperial blue Stilton, and another craved the fragrant boon of Caprera. There were fourteen little ones then, and consequently there were diverse opinions as to the kind of gift which Santa Claus should best bring; still, there was, as you can readily understand, an enthusiastic unanimity upon this point, namely, that the gift should be cheese of some brand or other.

"'My dears,' said our mother, 'what matters it whether the boon which Santa Claus brings be royal English cheddar or fromage de Bricquebec, Vermont sage, or Herkimer County skim-milk? We should be content with whatsoever Santa Claus bestows, so long as it be cheese, disjoined from all traps whatsoever, unmixed with Paris green, and free from glass, strychnine, and other harmful ingredients. As for myself, I shall be satisfied with a cut of nice, fresh Western reserve; for truly I recognize in no other viand or edible half the fragrance or half the gustfulness to be met with in one of these pale but aromatic domestic products. So run away to your dreams now, that Santa Claus may find you sleeping.'

"The children obeyed,—all but Squeaknibble. 'Let the others think what they please,' said she, 'but I don't believe in Santa Claus. I'm not going to bed, either. I'm going to creep out of this dark hole and have a quiet romp, all by myself, in the moonlight.' Oh, what a vain, foolish, wicked little mouse was Squeaknibble! But I will not reproach the dead; her punishment came all too swiftly. Now listen: who do you suppose overheard her talking so disrespectfully of Santa Claus?"

"Why, Santa Claus himself," said the old clock.

"Oh, no," answered the little mauve mouse. "It was that wicked, murderous cat! Just as Satan lurks and lies in wait for bad children, so does the cruel cat lurk and lie in wait for naughty little mice. And you can depend upon it that, when that awful cat heard Squeaknibble speak so disrespectfully of Santa Claus, her wicked eyes glowed with joy, her sharp teeth watered, and her bristling fur emitted electric sparks as big as marrowfat peas. Then what did that blood-thirsty monster do but scuttle as fast as she could into Dear-my-Soul's room, leap up into Dear-my-Soul's crib, and walk off with the pretty little white muff which Dear-my-Soul used to wear when she went for a visit to the little girl in the next block! What upon earth did the horrid old cat want with Dear-my-Soul's pretty little white muff? Ah, the duplicity, the diabolical ingenuity of that cat! Listen.

"In the first place," resumed the little mauve mouse, after a pause that testified eloquently to the depth of her emotion,—"in the first place, that wretched cat dressed herself up in that pretty little white muff, by which you are to understand that she crawled through the muff just so far as to leave her four cruel legs at liberty."

"Yes, I understand," said the old clock.

"Then she put on the boy doll's fur cap," said the little mauve mouse, "and when she was arrayed in the boy doll's fur cap and Dear-my-Soul's pretty little white muff, of course she didn't look like a cruel cat at all. But whom did she look like?"

"Like the boy doll," suggested the old clock.

"No, no!" cried the little mauve mouse.

"Like Dear-my-Soul?" asked the old clock.

"How stupid you are!" exclaimed the little mauve mouse. "Why, she looked like Santa Claus, of course!"

"Oh, yes; I see," said the old clock. "Now I begin to be interested; go on."

"Alas!" sighed the little mauve mouse, "not much remains to be told; but there is more of my story left than there was of Squeaknibble when that horrid cat crawled out of that miserable disguise. You are to understand that, contrary to her sagacious mother's injunction, and in notorious derision of the mooted coming of Santa Claus, Squeaknibble issued from the friendly hole in the chimney corner, and gambolled about over this very carpet, and, I dare say, in this very moonlight."

"I do not know," said the moonbeam, faintly. "I am so very old, and I have seen so many things—I do not know."

"Right merrily was Squeaknibble gambolling," continued the little mauve mouse, "and she had just turned a double back somersault without the use of what remained of her tail, when, all of a sudden, she beheld, looming up like a monster ghost, a figure all in white fur! Oh, how frightened she was, and how her little heart did beat! 'Purr, purr-r-r,' said the ghost in white fur. 'Oh, please don't hurt me!' pleaded Squeaknibble. 'No; I'll not hurt you,' said the ghost in white fur; 'I'm Santa Claus, and I've brought you a beautiful piece of savory old cheese, you dear little mousie, you.' Poor Squeaknibble was deceived; a sceptic all her life, she was at last befooled by the most palpable and most fatal of frauds. 'How good of you!' said Squeaknibble. 'I didn't believe there was a Santa Claus, and—' but before she could say more she was seized by two sharp, cruel claws that conveyed her crushed body to the murderous mouth of mousedom's most malignant foe. I can dwell no longer upon this harrowing scene. Suffice it to say that ere the morrow's sun rose like a big yellow Herkimer County cheese upon the spot where that tragedy had been enacted, poor Squeaknibble passed to that bourn whence two inches of her beautiful tail had preceded her by the space of three weeks to a day. As for Santa Claus, when he came that Christmas eve, bringing morceaux de Brie and of Stilton for the other little mice, he heard with sorrow of Squeaknibble's fate; and ere he departed he said that in all his experience he had never known of a mouse or of a child that had prospered after once saying that he didn't believe in Santa Claus."

"Well, that is a remarkable story," said the old clock. "But if you believe in Santa Claus, why aren't you in bed?"

"That's where I shall be presently," answered the little mauve mouse, "but I must have my scamper, you know. It is very pleasant, I assure you, to frolic in the light of the moon; only I cannot understand why you are always so cold and so solemn and so still, you pale, pretty little moonbeam."

"Indeed, I do not know that I am so," said the moonbeam. "But I am very old, and I have travelled many, many leagues, and I have seen wondrous things. Sometimes I toss upon the ocean, sometimes I fall upon a slumbering flower, sometimes I rest upon a dead child's face. I see the fairies at their play, and I hear mothers singing lullabies. Last night I swept across the frozen bosom of a river. A woman's face looked up at me; it was the picture of eternal rest. 'She is sleeping,' said the frozen river. 'I rock her to and fro, and sing to her. Pass gently by, O moonbeam; pass gently by, lest you awaken her.'"

"How strangely you talk," said the old clock. "Now, I'll warrant me that, if you wanted to, you could tell many a pretty and wonderful story. You must know many a Christmas tale; pray, tell us one to wear away this night of Christmas watching."

"I know but one," said the moonbeam. "I have told it over and over again, in every land and in every home; yet I do not weary of it. It is very simple. Should you like to hear it?"

"Indeed we should," said the old clock; "but before you begin, let me strike twelve; for I shouldn't want to interrupt you."

When the old clock had performed this duty with somewhat more than usual alacrity, the moonbeam began its story:—

"Upon a time—so long ago that I can't tell how long ago it was—I fell upon a hillside. It was in a far distant country; this I know, because, although it was the Christmas time, it was not in that country as it is wont to be in countries to the north. Hither the snow-king never came; flowers bloomed all the year, and at all times the lambs found pleasant pasturage on the hillsides. The night wind was balmy, and there was a fragrance of cedar in its breath. There were violets on the hillside, and I fell amongst them and lay there. I kissed them, and they awakened. 'Ah, is it you, little moonbeam?' they said, and they nestled in the grass which the lambs had left uncropped.

"A shepherd lay upon a broad stone on the hillside; above him spread an olive-tree, old, ragged, and gloomy; but now it swayed its rusty branches majestically in the shifting air of night. The shepherd's name was Benoni. Wearied with long watching, he had fallen asleep; his crook had slipped from his hand. Upon the hillside, too, slept the shepherd's flock. I had counted them again and again; I had stolen across their gentle faces and brought them pleasant dreams of green pastures and of cool water-brooks. I had kissed old Benoni, too, as he lay slumbering there; and in his dreams he seemed to see Israel's King come upon earth, and in his dreams he murmured the promised Messiah's name.

"'Ah, is it you, little moonbeam?' quoth the violets. 'You have come in good time. Nestle here with us, and see wonderful things come to pass.'

"'What are these wonderful things of which you speak?' I asked.

"'We heard the old olive-tree telling of them to-night,' said the violets. 'Do not go to sleep, little violets,' said the old olive-tree, 'for this is Christmas night, and the Master shall walk upon the hillside in the glory of the midnight hour.' So we waited and watched; one by one the lambs fell asleep; one by one the stars peeped out; the shepherd nodded and crooned and crooned and nodded, and at last he, too, went fast asleep, and his crook slipped from his keeping. Then we called to the old olive-tree yonder, asking how soon the midnight hour would come; but all the old olive-tree answered was 'Presently, presently,' and finally we, too, fell asleep, wearied by our long watching, and lulled by the rocking and swaying of the old olive-tree in the breezes of the night.

"'But who is this Master?' I asked.

"'A child, a little child,' they answered. 'He is called the little Master by the others. He comes here often, and plays among the flowers of the hillside. Sometimes the lambs, gambolling too carelessly, have crushed and bruised us so that we lie bleeding and are like to die; but the little Master heals our wounds and refreshes us once again.'

"I marvelled much to hear these things. 'The midnight hour is at hand,' said I, 'and I will abide with you to see this little Master of whom you speak.' So we nestled among the verdure of the hillside, and sang songs one to another.

"'Come away!' called the night wind; 'I know a beauteous sea not far hence, upon whose bosom you shall float, float, float away out into the mists and clouds, if you will come with me.'

"But I hid under the violets and amid the tall grass, that the night wind might not woo me with its pleading. 'Ho, there, old olive-tree!' cried the violets; 'do you see the little Master coming? Is not the midnight hour at hand?'

"'I can see the town yonder,' said the old olive-tree. 'A star beams bright over Bethlehem, the iron gates swing open, and the little Master comes.'

"Two children came to the hillside. The one, older than his comrade, was Dimas, the son of Benoni. He was rugged and sinewy, and over his brown shoulders was flung a goatskin; a leathern cap did not confine his long, dark curly hair. The other child was he whom they called the little Master; about his slender form clung raiment white as snow, and around his face of heavenly innocence fell curls of golden yellow. So beautiful a child I had not seen before, nor have I ever since seen such as he. And as they came together to the hillside, there seemed to glow about the little Master's head a soft white light, as if the moon had sent its tenderest, fairest beams to kiss those golden curls.

"'What sound was that?' cried Dimas, for he was exceeding fearful.

"'Have no fear, Dimas,' said the little Master. 'Give me thy hand, and I will lead thee.'

"Presently they came to the rock whereon Benoni, the shepherd, lay; and they stood under the old olive-tree, and the old olive-tree swayed no longer in the night wind, but bent its branches reverently in the presence of the little Master. It seemed as if the wind, too, stayed in its shifting course just then; for suddenly there was a solemn hush, and you could hear no noise, except that in his dreams Benoni spoke the Messiah's name.

"'Thy father sleeps,' said the little Master, 'and it is well that it is so; for that I love thee, Dimas, and that thou shalt walk with me in my Father's kingdom, I would show thee the glories of my birthright.'

"Then all at once sweet music filled the air, and light, greater than the light of day, illumined the sky and fell upon all that hillside. The heavens opened, and angels, singing joyous songs, walked to the earth. More wondrous still, the stars, falling from their places in the sky, clustered upon the old olive-tree, and swung hither and thither like colored lanterns. The flowers of the hillside all awakened, and they, too, danced and sang. The angels, coming hither, hung gold and silver and jewels and precious stones upon the old olive, where swung the stars; so that the glory of that sight, though I might live forever, I shall never see again. When Dimas heard and saw these things he fell upon his knees, and catching the hem of the little Master's garment, he kissed it.

"'Greater joy than this shall be thine, Dimas,' said the little Master; 'but first must all things be fulfilled.'

"All through that Christmas night did the angels come and go with their sweet anthems; all through that Christmas night did the stars dance and sing; and when it came my time to steal away, the hillside was still beautiful with the glory and the music of heaven."

"Well, is that all?" asked the old clock.

"No," said the moonbeam; "but I am nearly done. The years went on. Sometimes I tossed upon the ocean's bosom, sometimes I scampered o'er a battle-field, sometimes I lay upon a dead child's face. I heard the voices of Darkness and mothers' lullabies and sick men's prayers,—and so the years went on.

"I fell one night upon a hard and furrowed face. It was of ghostly pallor. A thief was dying on the cross, and this was his wretched face. About the cross stood men with staves and swords and spears, but none paid heed unto the thief. Somewhat beyond this cross another was lifted up, and upon it was stretched a human body my light fell not upon. But I heard a voice that somewhere I had heard before,—though where I did not know,—and this voice blessed those that railed and jeered and shamefully entreated. And suddenly the voice called 'Dimas, Dimas!' and the thief upon whose hardened face I rested made answer.

"Then I saw that it was Dimas; yet to this wicked criminal there remained but little of the shepherd child whom I had seen in all his innocence upon the hillside. Long years of sinful life had seared their marks into his face; yet now, at the sound of that familiar voice, somewhat of the old-time boyish look came back, and in the yearning of the anguished eyes I seemed to see the shepherd's son again.

"'The Master!' cried Dimas, and he stretched forth his neck that he might see him that spake.

"'O Dimas, how art thou changed!' cried the Master, yet there was in his voice no tone of rebuke save that which cometh of love.

"Then Dimas wept, and in that hour he forgot his pain. And the Master's consoling voice and the Master's presence there wrought in the dying criminal such a new spirit, that when at last his head fell upon his bosom, and the men about the cross said that he was dead, it seemed as if I shined not upon a felon's face, but upon the face of the gentle shepherd lad, the son of Benoni.

"And shining on that dead and peaceful face, I bethought me of the little Master's words that he had spoken under the old olive-tree upon the hillside: 'Your eyes behold the promised glory now, O Dimas,' I whispered, 'for with the Master you walk in Paradise.'"

Ah, little Dear-my-Soul, you know—you know whereof the moonbeam spake. The shepherd's bones are dust, the flocks are scattered, the old olive-tree is gone, the flowers of the hillside are withered, and none knoweth where the grave of Dimas is made. But last night, again, there shined a star over Bethlehem, and the angels descended from the sky to earth, and the stars sang together in glory. And the bells,—hear them, little Dear-my-Soul, how sweetly they are ringing,—the bells bear us the good tidings of great joy this Christmas morning, that our Christ is born, and that with him he bringeth peace on earth and good-will toward men.

CHAPTER V

THE DIVELL'S CHRYSTMASS

It befell that on a time ye Divell did walk to and fro upon ye earth, having in his mind full evill cogitations how that he might do despight; for of soche nature is ye Divell, and ever hath been, that continually doth he go about among men, being so dispositioned that it sufficeth him not that men sholde of their own forwardness, and by cause of the guile born in them, turn unto his wickedness, but rather that he sholde by his crewel artifices and diabolical machinations tempt them at all times and upon every hand to do his fiendly plaisaunce.

But it so fortuned that this time wherein ye Divell so walked upon ye earth was ye Chrystmass time; and wit ye well that how evill soever ye harte of man ben at other seasons, it is tofilled at ye Chrystmass time with charity and love, like as if it ben sanctified by ye exceeding holiness of that feast. Leastwise, this moche we know, that, whereas at other times envy and worldliness do prevail, for a verity our natures are toched at ye Chrystmass time as by ye hand of divinity, and conditioned for merciful deeds unto our fellow kind. Right wroth was ye Divell, therefore, when that he knew this ben ye Chrystmass time. And as rage doth often confirm in ye human harte an evill purpose, so was ye Divell now more diabolically minded to work his unclean will, and full hejeously fell he to roar and lash his ribald legs with his poyson taile. But ye Divell did presently conceive that naught might he accomplish by this means, since that men, affrighted by his roaring and astonied by ye fumes of brimstone and ye sulphur flames issuing from his mouth, wolde flee therefrom; whereas by subtile craft and by words of specious guile it more frequently befalls that ye Divell seduceth men and lureth them into his toils. So then ye Divell did in a little season feign to be in a full plaisaunt mind and of sweet purpose; and when that he had girt him about with an hermit's cloak, so that none might see his cloven feet and his poyson taile, right briskly did he fare him on his journey, and he did sing ye while a plaisaunt tune, like he had ben full of joyous contentation.

Now it befell that presently in his journey he did meet with a frere, Dan Dennyss, an holy man that fared him to a neighboring town for deeds of charity and godliness. Unto him spake ye Divell full courteysely, and required of him that he might bear him company; to which ye frere gave answer in seemly wise, that, if so be that he ben of friendly disposition, he wolde make him joy of his companionship and conversation. Then, whiles that they journeyed together, began ye Divell to discourse of theologies and hidden mysteries, and of conjurations, and of negromancy and of magick, and of Chaldee, and of astrology, and of chymistry, and of other occult and forbidden sciences, wherein ye Divell and all that ply his damnable arts are mightily learned and practised. Now wit ye well that this frere, being an holy man and a simple, and having an eye single to ye blessed works of his calling, was presently mightily troubled in his mind by ye artifices of ye Divell, and his harte began to waver and to be filled with miserable doubtings; for knowing nothing of ye things whereof ye Divell spake, he colde not make answer thereto, nor, being of godly cogitation and practice, had he ye confutations wherewith to meet ye abhominable argumentations of ye fiend.

Yet (and now shall I tell you of a special Providence) it did fortune, whiles yet ye Divell discoursed in this profane wise, there was vouchsafed unto ye frere a certain power to resist ye evill that environed him; for of a sodaine he did cast his doubtings and his misgivings to ye winds, and did fall upon ye Divell and did buffet him full sore, crying, "Thou art ye Divell! Get thee gone!" And ye frere plucked ye cloake from ye Divell and saw ye cloven feet and ye poyson taile, and straightway ye Divell ran roaring away. But ye frere fared upon his journey, for that he had had a successful issue from this grevious temptation, with thanksgiving and prayse.

Next came ye Divell into a town wherein were many people going to and fro upon works of charity, and doing righteous practices; and sorely did it repent ye Divell when that he saw ye people bent upon ye giving of alms and ye doing of charitable deeds. Therefore with mighty diligence did ye Divell apply himself to poyson ye minds of ye people, shewing unto them in artful wise how that by idleness or by righteous dispensation had ye poore become poore, and that, soche being ye will of God, it was an evill and rebellious thing against God to seeke to minister consolation unto these poore peoples. Soche like specious argumentations did ye Divell use to gain his diabolical ends; but by means of a grace whereof none then knew ye source, these men and these women unto whom ye Divell spake his hejeous heresies presently discovered force to withstand these fiendly temptations, and to continue in their Chrystianly practices, to ye glory of their faith and to ye benefite of ye needy, but to ye exceeding discomfiture of ye Divell; for ye which discomfiture I do give hearty thanks, and so also shall all of you, if so be that your hartes within you be of rightful disposition.

All that day long fared ye Divell to and fro among ye people of ye town, but none colde he bring into his hellish way of cogitation. Nor do I count this to be a marvellous thing; for, as I myself have herein shewn and as eche of us doth truly know, how can there be a place for ye Divell upon earth during this Chrystmass time when in ye very air that we breathe abideth a certain love and concord sent of heaven for the controul and edification of mankind, filling human hartes with peace and inclining human hands to ye delectable and blessed employments of charity? Nay, but you shall know that all this very season whereof I speak ye holy Chrystchilde himself did follow ye Divell upon earth, forefending the crewel evills which ye Divell fain wolde do and girding with confidence and love ye else frail natures of men. Soothly it is known of common report among you that when ye Chrystmass season comes upon ye earth there cometh with it also the spirit of our Chryst himself, that in ye similitude of a little childe descendeth from heaven and walketh among men. And if so be that by any chance ye Divell is minded to issue from his foul pit at soche a time, wit ye well that wheresoever ye fiend fareth to do his diabolical plaisaunce there also close at hand followeth ye gentle Chrystchilde; so that ye Divell, try how hard soever he may, hath no power at soche a time over the hartes of men.

Nay, but you shall know furthermore that of soche sweete quality and of so great efficacy is this heavenly spirit of charity at ye Chrystmass season, that oftentimes is ye Divell himself made to do a kindly deed. So at this time of ye which I you tell, ye Divell, walking upon ye earth with evill purpose, become finally overcome by ye gracious desire to give an alms; but nony alms had ye Divell to give, sith it is wisely ordained that ye Divell's offices shall be confined to his domain. Right grievously tormented therefore was ye Divell, in that he had nought of alms to bestow; but when presently he did meet with a beggar childe that besought him charity, ye Divell whipped out a knife and cut off his own taile, which taile ye Divell gave to ye beggar childe, for he had not else to give for a lyttle trinket toy to make merry with. Now wit ye well that this poyson instrument brought no evill to ye beggar childe, for by a sodaine miracle it ben changed into a flowre of gold, ye which gave great joy unto ye beggar childe and unto all them that saw this miracle how that it had ben wrought, but not by ye Divell. Then returned ye Divell unto his pit of fire; and since that day, whereupon befell this thing of which I speak, ye Divell hath had nony taile at all, as you that hath scene ye same shall truly testify.

But all that day long walked ye Chrystchilde upon ye earth, unseen to ye people but toching their hartes with his swete love and turning their hands to charity; and all felt that ye Chrystchilde was with them. So it was plaisaunt to do ye Chrystchilde's will, to succor ye needy, to comfort ye afflicted, and to lift up ye oppressed. Most plaisauntest of all was it to make merry with ye lyttle children, sithence of soche is ye kingdom whence ye Chrystchilde cometh.

Behold, ye season is again at hand; once more ye snows of winter lie upon all ye earth, and all Chrystantie is arrayed to the holy feast.

Presently shall ye star burn with exceeding brightness in ye east, ye sky shall be full of swete music, ye angels shall descend to earth with singing, and ye bells—ye joyous Chrystmass bells—shall tell us of ye babe that was born in Bethlehem.

Come to us now, O gentle Chrystchilde, and walke among us peoples of ye earth; enwheel us round about with thy protecting care; forefend all envious thoughts and evil deeds; toche thou our hearts with the glory of thy love, and quicken us to practices of peace, good-will, and charity meet for thy approval and acceptation.

CHAPTER VI

THE MOUNTAIN AND THE SEA

Once upon a time the air, the mountain, and the sea lived undisturbed upon all the earth. The mountain alone was immovable; he stood always here upon his rocky foundation, and the sea rippled and foamed at his feet, while the air danced freely over his head and about his grim face. It came to pass that both the sea and the air loved the mountain, but the mountain loved the sea.

"Dance on forever, O air," said the mountain; "dance on and sing your merry songs. But I love the gentle sea, who in sweet humility crouches at my feet or playfully dashes her white spray against my brown bosom."

Now the sea was full of joy when she heard these words, and her thousand voices sang softly with delight. But the air was filled with rage and jealousy, and she swore a terrible revenge.

"The mountain shall not wed the sea," muttered the envious air. "Enjoy your triumph while you may, O slumberous sister; I will steal you from your haughty lover!"

And it came to pass that ever after that the air each day caught up huge parts of the sea and sent them floating forever through the air in the shape of clouds. So each day the sea receded from the feet of the mountain, and her tuneful waves played no more around his majestic base.

"Whither art thou going, my love?" cried the mountain, in dismay.

"She is false to thee," laughed the air, mockingly. "She is going to another love far away."

But the mountain would not believe it. He towered his head aloft and cried more beseechingly than before: "Oh, whither art thou going, my beloved? I do not hear thy sweet voice, nor do thy soft white arms compass me about."

Then the sea cried out in an agony of helpless love. But the mountain heard her not, for the air refused to bring the words she said.

"She is false!" whispered the air. "I alone am true to thee."

But the mountain believed her not. Day after day he reared his massive head aloft and turned his honest face to the receding sea and begged her to return; day after day the sea threw up her snowy arms and uttered the wildest lamentations, but the mountain heard her not; and day by day the sea receded farther and farther from the mountain's base. Where she once had spread her fair surface appeared fertile plains and verdant groves all peopled with living things, whose voices the air brought to the mountain's ears in the hope that they might distract the mountain from his mourning.

But the mountain would not be comforted; he lifted his sturdy head aloft, and his sorrowing face was turned ever toward the fleeting object of his love. Hills, valleys, forests, plains, and other mountains separated them now, but over and beyond them all he could see her fair face lifted pleadingly toward him, while her white arms tossed wildly to and fro. But he did not know what words she said, for the envious air would not bear her messages to him.

Then many ages came and went, until now the sea was far distant, so very distant that the mountain could not behold her,—nay, had he been ten thousand times as lofty he could not have seen her, she was so far away. But still, as of old, the mountain stood with his majestic head high in the sky, and his face turned whither he had seen her fading like a dream away.

"Come back, come back, O my beloved!" he cried and cried.

And the sea, a thousand miles or more away, still thought forever of the mountain. Vainly she peered over the western horizon for a glimpse of his proud head and honest face. The horizon was dark. Her lover was far beyond; forests, plains, hills, valleys, rivers, and other mountains intervened. Her watching was as hopeless as her love.

"She is false!" whispered the air to the mountain. "She is false, and she has gone to another lover. I alone am true!"

But the mountain believed her not. And one day clouds came floating through the sky and hovered around the mountain's crest.

"Who art thou," cried the mountain,—"who art thou that thou fill'st me with such a subtile consolation? Thy breath is like my beloved's, and thy kisses are like her kisses."

"We come from the sea," answered the clouds. "She loves thee, and she has sent us to bid thee be courageous, for she will come back to thee."

Then the clouds covered the mountain and bathed him with the glory of the sea's true love. The air raged furiously, but all in vain. Ever after that the clouds came each day with love-messages from the sea, and oftentimes the clouds bore back to the distant sea the tender words the mountain spoke.

And so the ages come and go, the mountain rearing his giant head aloft, and his brown, honest face turned whither the sea departed; the sea stretching forth her arms to the distant mountain and repeating his dear name with her thousand voices.

Stand on the beach and look upon the sea's majestic calm and hear her murmurings; or see her when, in the frenzy of her hopeless love, she surges wildly and tosses her white arms and shrieks,— then you shall know how the sea loves the distant mountain.

The mountain is old and sear; the storms have beaten upon his breast, and great scars and seams and wrinkles are on his sturdy head and honest face. But he towers majestically aloft, and he looks always toward the distant sea and waits for her promised coming.

And so the ages come and go, but love is eternal.

CHAPTER VII

THE ROBIN AND THE VIOLET

Once upon a time a robin lived in the greenwood. Of all the birds his breast was the brightest, his music was the sweetest, and his life was the merriest. Every morning and evening he perched himself among the berries of the linden-tree, and carolled a song that made the whole forest joyous; and all day long he fluttered among the flowers and shrubbery of the wild-wood, and twittered gayly to the brooks, the ferns, and the lichens.

A violet grew among the mosses at the foot of the linden-tree where lived the robin. She was so very tiny and so very modest that few knew there was such a pretty little creature in the world. Withal she was so beautiful and so gentle that those who knew the violet loved her very dearly.

The south wind came wooing the violet. He danced through the shrubbery and ferns, and lingered on the velvet moss where the little flower grew. But when he kissed her pretty face and whispered to her, she hung her head and said, "No, no; it cannot be."

"Nay, little violet, do not be so cruel," pleaded the south wind; "let me bear you as my bride away to my splendid home in the south, where all is warmth and sunshine always."

But the violet kept repeating, "No, it cannot be; no, it cannot be," till at last the south wind stole away with a very heavy heart.

And the rose exclaimed, in an outburst of disgustful indignation: "What a foolish violet! How silly of her to refuse such a wooer as the south wind, who has a beautiful home and a patrimony of eternal warmth and sunshine!"

But the violet, as soon as the south wind had gone, looked up at the robin perched in the linden-tree and singing his clear song; and it seemed as if she blushed and as if she were thrilled with a great emotion as she beheld him. But the robin did not see the violet. His eyes were turned the other way, and he sang to the clouds in the sky.

The brook o'erleapt its banks one day, and straying toward the linden-tree, it was amazed at the loveliness of the violet. Never had it seen any flower half so beautiful.

"Oh, come and be my bride," cried the brook. "I am young and small now, but presently you shall see me grow to a mighty river whose course no human power can direct, and whose force nothing can resist. Cast thyself upon my bosom, sweet violet, and let us float together to that great destiny which awaits me."

But the violet shuddered and recoiled and said: "Nay, nay, impetuous brook, I will not be your bride." So, with many murmurs and complaints, the brook crept back to its jealous banks and resumed its devious and prattling way to the sea.

"Bless me!" cried the daisy, "only to think of that silly violet's refusing the brook! Was there ever another such piece of folly! Where else is there a flower that would not have been glad to go upon such a wonderful career? Oh, how short-sighted some folks are!"

But the violet paid no heed to these words; she looked steadfastly up into the foliage of the linden-tree where the robin was carolling. The robin did not see the violet; he was singing to the tops of the fir-trees over yonder.

The days came and went. The robin sang and fluttered in the greenwood, and the violet bided among the mosses at the foot of the linden; and although the violet's face was turned always upward to where the robin perched and sang, the robin never saw the tender little flower.

One day a huntsman came through the greenwood, and an arrow from his cruel bow struck the robin and pierced his heart. The robin was carolling in the linden, but his song was ended suddenly, and the innocent bird fell dying from the tree. "Oh, it is only a robin," said the huntsman, and with a careless laugh he went on his way.

The robin lay upon the mosses at the foot of the linden, close beside the violet. But he neither saw nor heard anything, for his life was nearly gone. The violet tried to bind his wound and stay the flow of his heart's blood, but her tender services were vain. The robin died without having seen her sweet face or heard her gentle voice.

Then the other birds of the greenwood came to mourn over their dead friend. The moles and the mice dug a little grave and laid the robin in it, after which the birds brought lichens and leaves, and covered the dead body, and heaped earth over all, and made a great lamentation. But when they went away, the violet remained; and after the sun had set, and the greenwood all was dark, the violet bent over the robin's grave and kissed it, and sang to the dead robin. And the violet watched by the robin's grave for weeks and months, her face pressed forward toward that tiny mound, and her gentle voice always singing softly and sweetly about the love she never had dared to tell.

Often after that the south wind and the brook came wooing her, but she never heard them, or, if she heard them, she did not answer. The vine that lived near the chestnut yonder said the violet was greatly changed; that from being a merry, happy thing, she had grown sad and reticent; she used to hold up her head as proudly as the others, but now she seemed broken and weary. The shrubs and flowers talked it all over many and many a time, but none of them could explain the violet's strange conduct.

It was autumn now, and the greenwood was not what it had been. The birds had flown elsewhere to be the guests of the storks during the winter months, the rose had run away to be the bride of the south wind, and the daisy had wedded the brook and was taking a bridal tour to the seaside watering-places. But the violet still lingered in the greenwood, and kept her vigil at the grave of the robin. She was pale and drooping, but still she watched and sang over the spot where her love lay buried. Each day she grew weaker and paler. The oak begged her to come and live among the warm lichens that protected him from the icy breath of the storm-king, but the violet chose to watch and sing over the robin's grave.

One morning, after a night of exceeding darkness and frost, the boisterous north wind came trampling through the greenwood.

"I have come for the violet," he cried; "she would not have my fair brother, but she must go with me, whether it pleases her or not!"

But when he came to the foot of the linden-tree his anger was changed to compassion. The violet was dead, and she lay upon the robin's grave. Her gentle face rested close to the little mound, as if, in her last moment, the faithful flower had stretched forth her lips to kiss the dust that covered her beloved.

CHAPTER VII

THE OAK-TREE AND THE IVY

In the greenwood stood a mighty oak. So majestic was he that all who came that way paused to admire his strength and beauty, and all the other trees of the greenwood acknowledged him to be their monarch.

Now it came to pass that the ivy loved the oak-tree, and inclining her graceful tendrils where he stood, she crept about his feet and twined herself around his sturdy and knotted trunk. And the oak-tree pitied the ivy.

"Oho!" he cried, laughing boisterously, but good-naturedly,—"oho! so you love me, do you, little vine? Very well, then; play about my feet, and I will keep the storms from you and will tell you pretty stories about the clouds, the birds, and the stars."

The ivy marvelled greatly at the strange stories the oak-tree told; they were stories the oak-tree heard from the wind that loitered about his lofty head and whispered to the leaves of his topmost branches. Sometimes the story was about the great ocean in the East, sometimes of the broad prairies in the West, sometimes of the ice-king who lived in the North, and sometimes of the flower-queen who dwelt in the South. Then, too, the moon told a story to the oak-tree every night,—or at least every night that she came to the greenwood, which was very often, for the greenwood is a very charming spot, as we all know. And the oak-tree repeated to the ivy every story the moon told and every song the stars sang.

"Pray, what are the winds saying now?" or "What song is that I hear?" the ivy would ask; and then the oak-tree would repeat the story or the song, and the ivy would listen in great wonderment.

Whenever the storms came, the oak-tree cried to the little ivy: "Cling close to me, and no harm shall befall you! See how strong I am; the tempest does not so much as stir me—I mock its fury!"

Then, seeing how strong and brave he was, the ivy hugged him closely; his brown, rugged breast protected her from every harm, and she was secure.

The years went by; how quickly they flew,—spring, summer, winter, and then again spring, summer, winter,—ah, life is short in the greenwood as elsewhere! And now the ivy was no longer a weakly little vine to excite the pity of the passer-by. Her thousand beautiful arms had twined hither and thither about the oak-tree, covering his brown and knotted trunk, shooting forth a bright, delicious foliage and stretching far up among his lower branches. Then the oak-tree's pity grew into a love for the ivy, and the ivy was filled with a great joy. And the oak-tree and the ivy were wed one June night, and there was a wonderful celebration in the greenwood; and there was the most beautiful music, in which the pine-trees, the crickets, the katydids, the frogs, and the nightingales joined with pleasing harmony.

The oak-tree was always good and gentle to the ivy. "There is a storm coming over the hills," he would say. "The east wind tells me so; the swallows fly low in the air, and the sky is dark. Cling close to me, my beloved, and no harm shall befall you."

Then, confidently and with an always-growing love, the ivy would cling more closely to the oak-tree, and no harm came to her.

"How good the oak-tree is to the ivy!" said the other trees of the greenwood. The ivy heard them, and she loved the oak-tree more and more. And, although the ivy was now the most umbrageous and luxuriant vine in all the greenwood, the oak-tree regarded her still as the tender little thing he had laughingly called to his feet that spring day, many years before,—the same little ivy he had told about the stars, the clouds, and the birds. And, just as patiently as in those days he had told her of these things, he now repeated other tales the winds whispered to his topmost boughs,—tales of the ocean in the East, the prairies in the West, the ice-king in the North, and the flower-queen in the South. Nestling upon his brave breast and in his stout arms, the ivy heard him tell these wondrous things, and she never wearied with the listening.

"How the oak-tree loves her!" said the ash. "The lazy vine has naught to do but to twine herself about the arrogant oak-tree and hear him tell his wondrous stories!"

The ivy heard these envious words, and they made her very sad; but she said nothing of them to the oak-tree, and that night the oak-tree rocked her to sleep as he repeated the lullaby a zephyr was singing to him.

"There is a storm coming over the hills," said the oak-tree one day. "The east wind tells me so; the swallows fly low in the air, and the sky is dark. Clasp me round about with thy dear arms, my beloved, and nestle close unto my bosom, and no harm shall befall thee."

"I have no fear," murmured the ivy; and she clasped her arms most closely about him and nestled unto his bosom.

The storm came over the hills and swept down upon the greenwood with deafening thunder and vivid lightning. The storm-king himself rode upon the blast; his horses breathed flames, and his chariot trailed through the air like a serpent of fire. The ash fell before the violence of the storm-king's fury, and the cedars groaning fell, and the hemlocks and the pines; but the oak-tree alone quailed not.

"Oho!" cried the storm-king, angrily, "the oak-tree does not bow to me, he does not tremble in my presence. Well, we shall see."

With that, the storm-king hurled a mighty thunderbolt at the oak-tree, and the brave, strong monarch of the greenwood was riven. Then, with a shout of triumph, the storm-king rode away.

"Dear oak-tree, you are riven by the storm-king's thunderbolt!" cried the ivy, in anguish.

"Ay," said the oak-tree, feebly, "my end has come; see, I am shattered and helpless."

"But I am unhurt," remonstrated the ivy, "and I will bind up your wounds and nurse you back to health and vigor."

And so it was that, although the oak-tree was ever afterward a riven and broken thing, the ivy concealed the scars upon his shattered form and covered his wounds all over with her soft foliage.

"I had hoped, dear one," she said, "to grow up to thy height, to live with thee among the clouds, and to hear the solemn voices thou didst hear. Thou wouldst have loved me better then?"

But the old oak-tree said: "Nay, nay, my beloved; I love thee better as thou art, for with thy beauty and thy love thou comfortest mine age."

Then would the ivy tell quaint stories to the old and broken oak-tree,—stories she had learned from the crickets, the bees, the butterflies, and the mice when she was an humble little vine and played at the foot of the majestic oak-tree, towering in the greenwood with no thought of the tiny shoot that crept toward him with her love. And these simple tales pleased the old and riven oak-tree; they were not as heroic as the tales the winds, the clouds, and the stars told, but they were far sweeter, for they were tales of contentment, of humility, of love.

So the old age of the oak-tree was grander than his youth.

And all who went through the greenwood paused to behold and admire the beauty of the oak-tree then; for about his seared and broken trunk the gentle vine had so entwined her graceful tendrils and spread her fair foliage, that one saw not the havoc of the years nor the ruin of the tempest, but only the glory of the oak-tree's age, which was the ivy's love and ministering.

CHAPTER IX

MARGARET: A PEARL

In a certain part of the sea, very many leagues from here, there once lived a large family of oysters noted for their beauty and size. But among them was one so small, so feeble, and so ill-looking as to excite the pity, if not the contempt, of all the others. The father, a venerable, bearded oyster, of august appearance and solemn deportment, was much mortified that one of his family should happen to be so sickly; and he sent for all the doctors in the sea to come and treat her; from which circumstance you are to note that doctors are an evil to be met with not alone upon terra firma. The first to come was Dr. Porpoise, a gentleman of the old school, who floundered around in a very important manner and was full of imposing ceremonies.

"Let me look at your tongue," said Dr. Porpoise, stroking his beard with one fin, impressively. "Ahem! somewhat coated, I see. And your pulse is far from normal; no appetite, I presume? Yes, my dear, your system is sadly out of order. You need medicine."

The little oyster hated medicine; so she cried,—yes, she actually shed cold, briny tears at the very thought of taking old Dr. Porpoise's prescriptions. But the father-oyster and the mother-oyster chided her sternly; they said that the medicine would be nice and sweet, and that the little oyster would like it. But the little oyster knew better than all that; yes, she knew a thing or two, even though she was only a little oyster.

Now Dr. Porpoise put a plaster on the little oyster's chest and a blister at her feet. He bade her eat nothing but a tiny bit of sea-foam on toast twice a day. Every two hours she was to take a spoonful of cod-liver oil, and before each meal a wineglassful of the essence of distilled cuttlefish. The plaster she didn't mind, but the blister and the cod-liver oil were terrible; and when it came to the essence of distilled cuttlefish—well, she just couldn't stand it! In vain her mother reasoned with her, and promised her a new doll and a skipping-rope and a lot of other nice things: the little oyster would have none of the horrid drug; until at last her father, abandoning his dignity in order to maintain his authority, had to hold her down by main strength and pour the medicine into her mouth. This was, as you will allow, quite dreadful.

But this treatment did the little oyster no good; and her parents made up their minds that they would send for another doctor, and one of a different school. Fortunately they were in a position to indulge in almost any expense, since the father-oyster himself was president of one of the largest banks of Newfoundland. So Dr. Sculpin came with his neat little medicine-box under his arm. And when he had looked at the sick little oyster's tongue, and had taken her temperature, and had felt her pulse, he said he knew what ailed her; but he did not tell anybody what it was. He threw away the plasters, the blisters, the cod-liver oil, and the essence of distilled cuttlefish, and said it was a wonder that the poor child had lived through it all!

"Will you please bring me two tumblerfuls of water?" he remarked to the mother-oyster.

The mother-oyster scuttled away, and soon returned with two conch-shells filled to the brim with pure, clear sea-water. Dr. Sculpin counted three grains of white sand into one shell, and three grains of yellow sand into the other shell, with great care.

"Now," said he to the mother-oyster, "I have numbered these 1 and 2. First, you are to give the patient ten drops out of No. 2, and in an hour after that, eight drops out of No. 1; the next hour, eight drops out of No. 2; and the next, or fourth, hour, ten drops out of No. 1. And so you are to continue hour by hour, until either the medicine or the child gives out."

"Tell me, doctor," asked the mother, "shall she continue the food suggested by Dr. Porpoise?"

"What food did he recommend?" inquired Dr. Sculpin.

"Sea-foam on toast," answered the mother.

Dr. Sculpin smiled a smile which seemed to suggest that Dr. Porpoise's ignorance was really quite annoying.

"My dear madam," said Dr. Sculpin, "the diet suggested by that quack, Porpoise, passed out of the books years ago. Give the child toast on sea-foam, if you wish to build up her debilitated forces."

Now, the sick little oyster did not object to this treatment; on the contrary, she liked it. But it did her no good. And one day, when she was feeling very dry, she drank both tumblerfuls of medicine, and it did not do her any harm; neither did it cure her: she remained the same sick little oyster,—oh, so sick! This pained her parents very much. They did not know what to do. They took her travelling; they gave her into the care of the eel for electric treatment; they sent her to the Gulf Stream for warm baths,—they tried everything, but to no avail. The sick little oyster remained a sick little oyster, and there was an end of it.

At last one day,—one cruel, fatal day,—a horrid, fierce-looking machine was poked down from the surface of the water far above, and with slow but intrepid movement began exploring every nook and crevice of the oyster village. There was not a family into which it did not intrude, nor a home circle whose sanctity it did not ruthlessly invade. It scraped along the great mossy rock; and lo! with a monstrous scratchy-te-scratch, the mother-oyster and the father-oyster and hundreds of other oysters were torn from their resting-places and borne aloft in a very jumbled and very frightened condition by the impertinent machine. Then down it came again, and the sick little oyster was among the number of those who were seized by the horrid monster this time. She found herself raised to the top of the sea; and all at once she was bumped in a boat, where she lay, puny and helpless, on a huge pile of other oysters. Two men were handling the fierce-looking machine. A little boy sat in the stern of the boat watching the huge pile of oysters. He was a pretty little boy, with bright eyes and long tangled hair. He wore no hat, and his feet were bare and brown.

"What a funny little oyster!" said the boy, picking up the sick little oyster; "it is no bigger than my thumb, and it is very pale."

"Throw it away," said one of the men. "Like as not it is bad and not fit to eat."

"No, keep it and send it out West for a Blue Point," said the other man,—what a heartless wretch he was!

But the little boy had already thrown the sick little oyster overboard. She fell in shallow water, and the rising tide carried her still farther toward shore, until she lodged against an old gum boot that lay half buried in the sand. There were no other oysters in sight. Her head ached and she was very weak; how lonesome, too, she was!—yet anything was better than being eaten,—at least so thought the little oyster, and so, I presume, think you.

For many weeks and many months the sick little oyster lay hard by the old gum boot; and in that time she made many acquaintances and friends among the crabs, the lobsters, the fiddlers, the star-fish, the waves, the shells, and the gay little fishes of the ocean. They did not harm her, for they saw that she was sick; they pitied her—some loved her. The one that loved her most was the perch with green fins that attended school every day in the academic shade of the big rocks in the quiet cove about a mile away. He was very gentle and attentive, and every afternoon he brought fresh cool sea-foam for the sick oyster to eat; he told her pretty stories, too,—stories which his grandmother, the venerable codfish, had told him of the sea king, the mermaids, the pixies, the water sprites, and the other fantastically beautiful dwellers in ocean-depths. Now while all this was very pleasant, the sick little oyster knew that the perch's wooing was hopeless, for she was very ill and helpless, and could never think of becoming a burden upon one so young and so promising as the gallant perch with green fins. But when she spoke to him in this strain, he would not listen; he kept right on bringing her more and more cool sea-foam every day.

The old gum boot was quite a motherly creature, and anon the sick little oyster became very much attached to her. Many times as the little invalid rested her aching head affectionately on the instep of the old gum boot, the old gum boot told her stories of the world beyond the sea: how she had been born in a mighty forest, and how proud her folks were of their family tree; how she had been taken from that forest and moulded into the shape she now bore; how she had graced and served a foot in amphibious capacities, until at last, having seen many things and having travelled much, she had been cast off and hurled into the sea to be the scorn of every crab and the derision of every fish. These stories were all new to the little oyster, and amazing, too; she knew only of the sea, having lived therein all her life. She in turn told the old gum boot quaint legends of the ocean,—the simple tales she had heard in her early home; and there was a sweetness and a simplicity in these stories of the deep that charmed the old gum boot, shrivelled and hardened and pessimistic though she was.

Yet, in spite of it all,—the kindness, the care, the amusements, and the devotion of her friends,—the little oyster remained always a sick and fragile thing. But no one heard her complain, for she bore her suffering patiently.

Not far from this beach where the ocean ended its long travels there was a city, and in this city there dwelt with her parents a maiden of the name of Margaret. From infancy she had been sickly, and although she had now reached the years of early womanhood, she could not run or walk about as others did, but she had to be wheeled hither and thither in a chair. This was very sad; yet Margaret was so gentle and uncomplaining that from aught she said you never would have thought her life was full of suffering. Seeing her helplessness, the sympathetic things of Nature had compassion and were very good to Margaret. The sunbeams stole across her pathway everywhere, the grass clustered thickest and greenest where she went, the winds caressed her gently as they passed, and the birds loved to perch near her window and sing their prettiest songs. Margaret loved them all,— the sunlight, the singing winds, the grass, the carolling birds. She communed with them; their wisdom inspired her life, and this wisdom gave her nature a rare beauty.

Every pleasant day Margaret was wheeled from her home in the city down to the beach, and there for hours she would sit, looking out, far out upon the ocean, as if she were communing with the ocean spirits that lifted up their white arms from the restless waters and beckoned her to come.

Oftentimes the children playing on the beach came where Margaret sat, and heard her tell little stories of the pebbles and the shells, of the ships away out at sea, of the ever-speeding gulls, of the grass, of the flowers, and of the other beautiful things of life; and so in time the children came to love Margaret. Among those who so often gathered to hear the gentle sick girl tell her pretty stories was a youth of Margaret's age,—older than the others, a youth with sturdy frame and a face full of candor and earnestness. His name was Edward, and he was a student in the city; he hoped to become a great scholar sometime, and he toiled very zealously to that end. The patience, the gentleness, the sweet simplicity, the fortitude of the sick girl charmed him. He found in her little stories a quaint and beautiful philosophy he never yet had found in books; there was a valor in her life he never yet had read of in the histories. So, every day she came and sat upon the beach, Edward came too; and with the children he heard Margaret's stories of the sea, the air, the grass, the birds, and the flowers.

From her moist eyrie in the surf the old gum boot descried the group upon the beach each pleasant day. Now the old gum boot had seen enough of the world to know a thing or two, as we presently shall see.

"That tall young man is not a child," quoth the old gum boot, "yet he comes every day with the children to hear the sick girl tell her stories! Ah, ha!"

"Perhaps he is the doctor," suggested the little oyster; and then she added with a sigh, "but, oh! I hope not."

This suggestion seemed to amuse the old gum boot highly; at least she fell into such hysterical laughter that she sprung a leak near her little toe, which, considering her environments, was a serious mishap.

"Unless I am greatly mistaken, my child," said the old gum boot to the little oyster, "that young man is in love with the sick girl!"

"Oh, how terrible!" said the little oyster; and she meant it too, for she was thinking of the gallant young perch with green fins.

"Well, I've said it, and I mean it!" continued the old gum boot; "now just wait and see."

The old gum boot had guessed aright—so much for the value of worldly experience! Edward loved Margaret; to him she was the most beautiful, the most perfect being in the world; her very words seemed to exalt his nature. Yet he never spoke to her of love. He was content to come with the children to hear her stories, to look upon her sweet face, and to worship her in silence. Was not that a very wondrous love?

In course of time the sick girl Margaret became more interested in the little ones that thronged daily to hear her pretty stories, and she put her beautiful fancies into the little songs and quaint poems and tender legends,—songs and poems and legends about the sea, the flowers, the birds, and the other beautiful creations of Nature; and in all there was a sweet simplicity, a delicacy, a reverence, that bespoke Margaret's spiritual purity and wisdom. In this teaching, and marvelling ever at its beauty, Edward grew to manhood. She was his inspiration, yet he never spoke of love to Margaret. And so the years went by.

Beginning with the children, the world came to know the sick girl's power. Her songs were sung in every home, and in every home her verses and her little stories were repeated. And so it was that Margaret came to be beloved of all, but he who loved her best spoke never of his love to her.

And as these years went by, the sick little oyster lay in the sea cuddled close to the old gum boot. She was wearier now than ever before, for there was no cure for her malady. The gallant perch with green fins was very sad, for his wooing had been hopeless. Still he was devoted, and still he came each day to the little oyster, bringing her cool sea-foam and other delicacies of the ocean. Oh, how sick the little oyster was! But the end came at last.

The children were on the beach one day, waiting for Margaret, and they wondered that she did not come. Presently, grown restless, many of the boys scampered into the water and stood there, with their trousers rolled up, boldly daring the little waves that rippled up from the overflow of the surf. And one little boy happened upon the old gum boot. It was a great discovery.

"See the old gum boot," cried the boy, fishing it out of the water and holding it on high. "And here is a little oyster fastened to it! How funny!"

The children gathered round the curious object on the beach. None of them had ever seen such a funny old gum boot, and surely none of them had ever seen such a funny little oyster. They tore the pale, knotted little thing from her foster-mother, and handled her with such rough curiosity that even had she been a robust oyster she must certainly have died. At any rate, the little oyster was dead now; and the bereaved perch with green fins must have known it, for he swam up and down his native cove disconsolately.

It befell in that same hour that Margaret lay upon her deathbed, and knowing that she had not long to live, she sent for Edward. And Edward, when he came to her, was filled with anguish, and clasping her hands in his, he told her of his love.

Then Margaret answered him: "I knew it, dear one; and all the songs I have sung and all the words I have spoken and all the prayers I have made have been with you, dear one,—all with you in my heart of hearts."

"You have purified and exalted my life," cried Edward; "you have been my best and sweetest inspiration; you have taught me the eternal truth,—you are my beloved!"

And Margaret said: "Then in my weakness hath there been a wondrous strength, and from my sufferings cometh the glory I have sought—"

So Margaret died, and like a broken lily she lay upon her couch; and all the sweetness of her pure and gentle life seemed to come down and rest upon her face; and the songs she had sung and the beautiful stories she had told were back, too, on angel wings, and made sweet music in that chamber.

The children were lingering on the beach when Edward came that day. He could hear them singing the songs Margaret had taught them. They wondered that he came alone.

"See," cried one of the boys, running to meet him and holding a tiny shell in his hand,—"see what we have found in this strange little shell. Is it not beautiful!"

Edward took the dwarfed, misshapen thing and lo! it held a beauteous pearl.

O little sister mine, let me look into your eyes and read an inspiration there; let me hold your thin white hand and know the strength of a philosophy more beautiful than human knowledge teaches; let me see in your dear, patient little face and hear in your gentle voice the untold valor of your suffering life. Come, little sister, let me fold you in my arms and have you ever with me, that in the glory of your faith and love I may walk the paths of wisdom and of peace.

CHAPTER X

THE SPRINGTIME

A child once said to his grandsire: "Gran'pa, what do the flowers mean when they talk to the old oak-tree about death? I hear them talking every day, but I cannot understand; it is all very strange."

The grandsire bade the child think no more of these things; the flowers were foolish prattlers,—what right had they to put such notions into a child's head? But the child did not do his grandsire's bidding; he loved the flowers and the trees, and he went each day to hear them talk.

It seems that the little vine down by the stone-wall had overheard the south wind say to the rosebush: "You are a proud, imperious beauty now, and will not listen to my suit; but wait till my boisterous brother comes from the North,—then you will droop and wither and die, all because you would not listen to me and fly with me to my home by the Southern sea."

These words set the little vine to thinking; and when she had thought for a long time she spoke to the daisy about it, and the daisy called in the violet, and the three little ones had a very serious conference; but, having talked it all over, they came to the conclusion that it was as much of a mystery as ever. The old oak-tree saw them.

"You little folks seem very much puzzled about something," said the old oak-tree.

"I heard the south wind tell the rosebush that she would die," exclaimed the vine, "and we do not understand what it is. Can you tell us what it is to die?"

The old oak-tree smiled sadly.

"I do not call it death," said the old oak-tree; "I call it sleep,—a long, restful, refreshing sleep."

"How does it feel?" inquired the daisy, looking very full of astonishment and anxiety.

"You must know," said the old oak-tree, "that after many, many days we all have had such merry times and have bloomed so long and drunk so heartily of the dew and sunshine and eaten so much of the goodness of the earth that we feel very weary and we long for repose. Then a great wind comes out of the north, and we shiver in its icy blast. The sunshine goes away, and there is no dew for us nor any nourishment in the earth, and we are glad to go to sleep."

"Mercy on me!" cried the vine, "I shall not like that at all! What, leave this smiling meadow and all the pleasant grass and singing bees and frolicsome butterflies? No, old oak-tree, I would never go to sleep; I much prefer sporting with the winds and playing with my little friends, the daisy and the violet."

"And I," said the violet, "I think it would be dreadful to go to sleep. What if we never should wake up again!"

The suggestion struck the others dumb with terror,—all but the old oak-tree.

"Have no fear of that," said the old oak-tree, "for you are sure to awaken again, and when you have awakened the new life will be sweeter and happier than the old."

"What nonsense!" cried the thistle. "You children shouldn't believe a word of it. When you go to sleep you die, and when you die there's the last of you!"

The old oak-tree reproved the thistle; but the thistle maintained his abominable heresy so stoutly that the little vine and the daisy and the violet were quite at a loss to know which of the two to believe,—the old oak-tree or the thistle.

The child heard it all and was sorely puzzled. What was this death, this mysterious sleep? Would it come upon him, the child? And after he had slept awhile would he awaken? His grandsire would not tell him of these things; perhaps his grandsire did not know.

It was a long, long summer, full of sunshine and bird-music, and the meadow was like a garden, and the old oak-tree looked down upon the grass and flowers and saw that no evil befell them. A long, long play-day it was to the little vine, the daisy, and the violet. The crickets and the grasshoppers and the bumblebees joined in the sport, and romped and made music till it seemed like an endless carnival. Only every now and then the vine and her little flower friends talked with the old oak-tree about that strange sleep and the promised awakening, and the thistle scoffed at the old oak-tree's cheering words. The child was there and heard it all.

One day the great wind came out of the north. Hurry-scurry! back to their warm homes in the earth and under the old stone-wall scampered the crickets and bumblebees to go to sleep. Whirr, whirr! Oh, but how piercing the great wind was; how different from his amiable brother who had travelled all the way from the Southern sea to kiss the flowers and woo the rose!

"Well, this is the last of us!" exclaimed the thistle; "we're going to die, and that's the end of it all!"

"No, no," cried the old oak-tree; "we shall not die; we are going to sleep. Here, take my leaves, little flowers, and you shall sleep warm under them. Then, when you awaken, you shall see how much sweeter and happier the new life is."

The little ones were very weary indeed. The promised sleep came very gratefully.

"We would not be so willing to go to sleep if we thought we should not awaken," said the violet.

So the little ones went to sleep. The little vine was the last of all to sink to her slumbers; she nodded in the wind and tried to keep awake till she saw the old oak-tree close his eyes, but her efforts were vain; she nodded and nodded, and bowed her slender form against the old stone-wall, till finally she, too, had sunk into repose. And then the old oak-tree stretched his weary limbs and gave a last look at the sullen sky and at the slumbering little ones at his feet; and with that, the old oak-tree fell asleep too.

The child saw all these things, and he wanted to ask his grandsire about them, but his grandsire would not tell him of them; perhaps his grandsire did not know.

The child saw the storm-king come down from the hills and ride furiously over the meadows and over the forest and over the town. The snow fell everywhere, and the north wind played solemn music in the chimneys. The storm-king put the brook to bed, and threw a great mantle of snow over him; and the brook that had romped and prattled all the summer and told pretty tales to the grass and flowers,—the brook went to sleep too. With all his fierceness and bluster, the storm-king was very kind; he did not awaken the old oak-tree and the slumbering flowers. The little vine lay under the fleecy snow against the old stone-wall and slept peacefully, and so did the violet and the daisy. Only the wicked old thistle thrashed about in his sleep as if he dreamt bad dreams, which, all will allow, was no more than he deserved.

All through that winter—and it seemed very long—the child thought of the flowers and the vine and the old oak-tree, and wondered whether in the springtime they would awaken from their sleep; and he wished for the springtime to come. And at last the springtime came. One day the sunbeams fluttered down from the sky and danced all over the meadow.

"Wake up, little friends!" cried the sunbeams,—"wake up, for it is the springtime!"

The brook was the first to respond. So eager, so fresh, so exuberant was he after his long winter sleep, that he leaped from his bed and frolicked all over the meadow and played all sorts of curious antics. Then a little bluebird was seen in the hedge one morning. He was calling to the violet.

"Wake up, little violet," called the bluebird. "Have I come all this distance to find you sleeping? Wake up; it is the springtime!"

That pretty little voice awakened the violet, of course.

"Oh, how sweetly I have slept!" cried the violet; "how happy this new life is! Welcome, dear friends!"

And presently the daisy awakened, fresh and beautiful, and then the little vine, and, last of all, the old oak-tree. The meadow was green, and all around there were the music, the fragrance, the new, sweet life of the springtime.

"I slept horribly," growled the thistle. "I had bad dreams. It was sleep, after all, but it ought to have been death."

The thistle never complained again; for just then a four-footed monster stalked through the meadow and plucked and ate the thistle and then stalked gloomily away; which was the last of the sceptical thistle,—truly a most miserable end!

"You said the truth, dear old oak-tree!" cried the little vine. "It was not death,—it was only a sleep, a sweet, refreshing sleep, and this awakening is very beautiful."

They all said so,—the daisy, the violet, the oak-tree, the crickets, the bees, and all the things and creatures of the field and forest that had awakened from their long sleep to swell the beauty and the glory of the springtime. And they talked with the child, and the child heard them. And although the grandsire never spoke to the child about these things, the child learned from the flowers and trees a lesson of the springtime which perhaps the grandsire never knew.

CHAPTER XI

RODOLPH AND HIS KING

"Tell me, Father," said the child at Rodolph's knee,—"tell me of the king."

"There is no king, my child," said Rodolph. "What you have heard are old women's tales. Do not believe them, for there is no king."

"But why, then," queried the child, "do all the people praise and call on him; why do the birds sing of the king; and why do the brooks always prattle his name, as they dance from the hills to the sea?"

"Nay," answered Rodolph, "you imagine these things; there is no king. Believe me, child, there is no king."

So spake Rodolph; but scarcely had he uttered the words when the cricket in the chimney corner chirped loudly, and his shrill notes seemed to say: "The king—the king." Rodolph could hardly believe his ears. How had the cricket learned to chirp these words? It was beyond all understanding. But still the cricket chirped, and still his musical monotone seemed to say, "The king—the king," until, with an angry frown, Rodolph strode from his house, leaving the child to hear the cricket's song alone.

But there were other voices to remind Rodolph of the king. The sparrows were fluttering under the eaves, and they twittered noisily as Rodolph strode along, "The king, king, king!" "The king, king, king," twittered the sparrows, and their little tones were full of gladness and praise.

A thrush sat in the hedge, and she was singing her morning song. It was a hymn of praise,—how beautiful it was! "The king—the king—the king," sang the thrush, and she sang, too, of his goodness,—it was a wondrous song, and it was all about the king.

The doves cooed in the elm-trees. "Sing to us!" cried their little ones, stretching out their pretty heads from the nests. Then the doves nestled hard by and murmured lullabies, and the lullabies were of the king who watched over and protected even the little birds in their nests.

Rodolph heard these things, and they filled him with anger.

"It is a lie!" muttered Rodolph; and in great petulance he came to the brook.

How noisy and romping the brook was; how capricious, how playful, how furtive! And how he called to the willows and prattled to the listening grass as he scampered on his way. But Rodolph turned aside and his face grew darker. He did not like the voice of the brook; for, lo! just as the cricket had chirped and the birds had sung, so did this brook murmur and prattle and sing ever of the king, the king, the king.

So, always after that, wherever Rodolph went, he heard voices that told him of the king; yes, even in their quiet, humble way, the flowers seemed to whisper the king's name, and every breeze that fanned his brow had a tale to tell of the king and his goodness.

"But there is no king!" cried Rodolph. "They all conspire to plague me! There is no king—there is no king!"

Once he stood by the sea and saw a mighty ship go sailing by. The waves plashed on the shore and told stories to the pebbles and the sands. Rodolph heard their thousand voices, and he heard them telling of the king.

Then a great storm came upon the sea, a tempest such as never before had been seen. The waves dashed mountain-high and overwhelmed the ship, and the giant voices of the winds and waves cried of the king, the king! The sailors strove in agony till all seemed lost. Then, when they could do no more, they stretched out their hands and called upon the king to save them,—the king, the king, the king!

Rodolph saw the tempest subside. The angry winds were lulled, and the mountain waves sank into sleep, and the ship came safely into port. Then the sailors sang a hymn of praise, and the hymn was of the king and to the king.

"But there is no king!" cried Rodolph. "It is a lie; there is no king!"

Yet everywhere he went he heard always of the king; the king's name and the king's praises were on every tongue; aye, and the things that had no voices seemed to wear the king's name written upon them, until Rodolph neither saw nor heard anything that did not mind him of the king.

Then, in great anger, Rodolph said: "I will go to the mountain-tops; there I shall find no birds, nor trees, nor brooks, nor flowers to prate of a monarch no one has ever seen. There shall there be no sea to vex me with its murmurings, nor any human voice to displease me with its superstitions."

So Rodolph went to the mountains, and he scaled the loftiest pinnacle, hoping that there at last he might hear no more of that king whom none had ever seen. And as he stood upon the pinnacle, what a mighty panorama was spread before him, and what a mighty anthem swelled upon his ears! The peopled plains, with their songs and murmurings, lay far below; on every side the mountain peaks loomed up in snowy grandeur; and overhead he saw the sky, blue, cold, and cloudless, from horizon to horizon.

What voice was that which spoke in Rodolph's bosom then as Rodolph's eyes beheld this revelation?

"There is a king!" said the voice. "The king lives, and this is his abiding-place!"

And how did Rodolph's heart stand still when he felt Silence proclaim the king,—not in tones of thunder, as the tempest had proclaimed him, nor in the singing voices of the birds and brooks, but so swiftly, so surely, so grandly, that Rodolph's soul was filled with awe ineffable.

Then Rodolph cried: "There is a king, and I acknowledge him! Henceforth my voice shall swell the songs of all in earth and air and sea that know and praise his name!"

So Rodolph went to his home. He heard the cricket singing of the king; yes, and the sparrows under the eaves, the thrush in the hedge, the doves in the elms, and the brook, too, all singing of the king; and Rodolph's heart was gladdened by their music. And all the earth and the things of the earth seemed more beautiful to Rodolph now that he believed in the king; and to the song all Nature sang Rodolph's voice and Rodolph's heart made harmonious response.

"There is a king, my child," said Rodolph to his little one. "Together let us sing to him, for he is our king, and his goodness abideth forever and forever."

CHAPTER XII

THE HAMPSHIRE HILLS

One afternoon many years ago two little brothers named Seth and Abner were playing in the orchard. They were not troubled with the heat of the August day, for a soft, cool wind came up from the river in the valley over yonder and fanned their red cheeks and played all kinds of pranks with their tangled curls. All about them was the hum of bees, the song of birds, the smell of clover, and the merry music of the crickets. Their little dog Fido chased them through the high, waving grass, and rolled with them under the trees, and barked himself hoarse in his attempt to keep pace with their laughter. Wearied at length, they lay beneath the bellflower-tree and looked off at the Hampshire hills, and wondered if the time ever would come when they should go out into the world beyond those hills and be great, noisy men. Fido did not understand it at all. He lolled in the grass, cooling his tongue on the clover bloom, and puzzling his brain to know why his little masters were so quiet all at once.

"I wish I were a man," said Abner, ruefully. "I want to be somebody and do something. It is very hard to be a little boy so long and to have no companions but little boys and girls, to see nothing but these same old trees and this same high grass, and to hear nothing but the same bird-songs from one day to another."

"That is true," said Seth. "I, too, am very tired of being a little boy, and I long to go out into the world and be a man like my gran'pa or my father or my uncles. With nothing to look at but those distant hills and the river in the valley, my eyes are wearied; and I shall be very happy when I am big enough to leave this stupid place."

Had Fido understood their words he would have chided them, for the little dog loved his home and had no thought of any other pleasure than romping through the orchard and playing with his little masters all the day. But Fido did not understand them.

The clover bloom heard them with sadness. Had they but listened in turn they would have heard the clover saying softly: "Stay with me while you may, little boys; trample me with your merry feet; let me feel the imprint of your curly heads and kiss the sunburn on your little cheeks. Love me while you may, for when you go away you never will come back."

The bellflower-tree heard them, too, and she waved her great, strong branches as if she would caress the impatient little lads, and she whispered: "Do not think of leaving me: you are children, and you know nothing of the world beyond those distant hills. It is full of trouble and care and sorrow; abide here in this quiet spot till you are prepared to meet the vexations of that outer world. We are for you,—we trees and grass and birds and bees and flowers. Abide with us, and learn the wisdom we teach."

The cricket in the raspberry-hedge heard them, and she chirped, oh! so sadly: "You will go out into the world and leave us and never think of us again till it is too late to return. Open your ears, little boys, and hear my song of contentment."

So spake the clover bloom and the bellflower-tree and the cricket; and in like manner the robin that nested in the linden over yonder, and the big bumblebee that lived in the hole under the pasture gate, and the butterfly and the wild rose pleaded with them, each in his own way; but the little boys did not heed them, so eager were their desires to go into and mingle with the great world beyond those distant hills.

Many years went by; and at last Seth and Abner grew to manhood, and the time was come when they were to go into the world and be brave, strong men. Fido had been dead a long time. They had made him a grave under the bellflower-tree,—yes, just where he had romped with the two little boys that August afternoon Fido lay sleeping amid the humming of the bees and the perfume of the clover. But Seth and Abner did not think of Fido now, nor did they give even a passing thought to any of their old friends,—the bellflower-tree, the clover, the cricket, and the robin. Their hearts beat with exultation. They were men, and they were going beyond the hills to know and try the world.

They were equipped for that struggle, not in a vain, frivolous way, but as good and brave young men should be. A gentle mother had counselled them, a prudent father had advised them, and they had gathered from the sweet things of Nature much of that wisdom before which all knowledge is as nothing. So they were fortified. They went beyond the hills and came into the West. How great and busy was the world,—how great and busy it was here in the West! What a rush and noise and turmoil and seething and surging, and how keenly did the brothers have to watch and struggle for vantage ground. Withal, they prospered; the counsel of the mother, the advice of the father, the wisdom of the grass and flowers and trees, were much to them, and they prospered. Honor and riches came to them, and they were happy. But amid it all, how seldom they thought of the little home among the circling hills where they had learned the first sweet lessons of life!

And now they were old and gray. They lived in splendid mansions, and all people paid them honor.

One August day a grim messenger stood in Seth's presence and beckoned to him.

"Who are you?" cried Seth. "What strange power have you over me that the very sight of you chills my blood and stays the beating of my heart?"

Then the messenger threw aside his mask, and Seth saw that he was Death. Seth made no outcry; he knew what the summons meant, and he was content. But he sent for Abner.

And when Abner came, Seth was stretched upon his bed, and there was a strange look in his eyes and a flush upon his cheeks, as though a fatal fever had laid hold on him.

"You shall not die!" cried Abner, and he threw himself about his brother's neck and wept.

But Seth bade Abner cease his outcry. "Sit here by my bedside and talk with me," said he, "and let us speak of the Hampshire hills."

A great wonder overcame Abner. With reverence he listened, and as he listened, a sweet peace seemed to steal into his soul.

"I am prepared for Death," said Seth, "and I will go with Death this day. Let us talk of our childhood now, for, after all the battle with this great world, it is pleasant to think and speak of our boyhood among the Hampshire hills."

"Say on, dear brother," said Abner.

"I am thinking of an August day long ago," said Seth, solemnly and softly. "It was so very long ago, and yet it seems only yesterday. We were in the orchard together, under the bellflower-tree, and our little dog—"

"Fido," said Abner, remembering it all, as the years came back.

"Fido and you and I, under the bellflower-tree," said Seth. "How we had played, and how weary we were, and how cool the grass was, and how sweet was the fragrance of the flowers! Can you remember it, brother?"

"Oh, yes," replied Abner, "and I remember how we lay among the clover and looked off at the distant hills and wondered of the world beyond."

"And amid our wonderings and longings," said Seth, "how the old bellflower-tree seemed to stretch her kind arms down to us as if she would hold us away from that world beyond the hills."

"And now I can remember that the clover whispered to us, and the cricket in the raspberry-hedge sang to us of contentment," said Abner.

"The robin, too, carolled in the linden."

"It is very sweet to remember it now," said Seth. "How blue and hazy the hills looked; how cool the breeze blew up from the river; how like a silver lake the old pickerel pond sweltered under the summer sun over beyond the pasture and broom-corn, and how merry was the music of the birds and bees!"

So these old men, who had been little boys together, talked of the August afternoon when with Fido they had romped in the orchard and rested beneath the bellflower-tree. And Seth's voice grew fainter, and his eyes were, oh! so dim; but to the very last he spoke of the dear old days and the orchard and the clover and the Hampshire hills. And when Seth fell asleep forever, Abner kissed his brother's lips and knelt at the bedside and said the prayer his mother had taught him.

In the street without there was the noise of passing carts, the cries of trades-people, and all the bustle of a great and busy city; but, looking upon Seth's dear, dead face, Abner could hear only the music voices of birds and crickets and summer winds as he had heard them with Seth when they were little boys together, back among the Hampshire hills.

CHAPTER XIII

EZRA'S THANKSGIVIN' OUT WEST

Ezra had written a letter to the home folks, and in it he had complained that never before had he spent such a weary, lonesome day as this Thanksgiving day had been. Having finished this letter, he sat for a long time gazing idly into the open fire that snapped cinders all over the hearthstone and sent its red forks dancing up the chimney to join the winds that frolicked and gambolled across the Kansas prairies that raw November night. It had rained hard all day, and was cold; and although the open fire made every honest effort to be cheerful, Ezra, as he sat in front of it in the wooden rocker and looked down into the glowing embers, experienced a dreadful feeling of loneliness and homesickness.

"I'm sick o' Kansas," said Ezra to himself. "Here I've been in this plaguey country for goin' on a year, and—yes, I'm sick of it, powerful sick of it. What a miser'ble Thanksgivin' this has been! They don't know what Thanksgivin' is out this way. I wish I was back in ol' Mass'chusetts—that's the country for me, and they hev the kind o' Thanksgivin' I like!"

Musing in this strain, while the rain went patter-patter on the window-panes, Ezra saw a strange sight in the fireplace,—yes, right among the embers and the crackling flames Ezra saw a strange, beautiful picture unfold and spread itself out like a panorama.

"How very wonderful!" murmured the young man. Yet he did not take his eyes away, for the picture soothed him and he loved to look upon it.

"It is a pictur' of long ago," said Ezra, softly. "I had like to forgot it, but now it comes back to me as nat'ral-like as an ol' friend. An' I seem to be a part of it, an' the feelin' of that time comes back with the pictur', too."

Ezra did not stir. His head rested upon his hand, and his eyes were fixed upon the shadows in the firelight.

"It is a pictur' of the ol' home," said Ezra to himself. "I am back there in Belchertown, with the Holyoke hills up north an' the Berkshire mountains a loomin' up gray an' misty-like in the western horizon. Seems as if it wuz early mornin'; everything is still, and it is so cold when we boys crawl out o' bed that, if it wuzn't Thanksgivin' mornin', we'd crawl back again an' wait for Mother to call us. But it is Thanksgivin' mornin', an' we're goin' skatin' down on the pond. The squealin' o' the pigs has told us it is five o'clock, and we must hurry; we're goin' to call by for the Dickerson boys an' Hiram Peabody, an' we've got to hyper! Brother Amos gets on about half o' my clo'es, and I get on 'bout half o' his, but it's all the same; they are stout, warm clo'es, and they're big enough to fit any of us boys,—Mother looked out for that when she made 'em. When we go downstairs we find the girls there, all bundled up nice an' warm,—Mary an' Helen an' Cousin Irene. They're goin' with us, an' we all start out tiptoe and quiet-like so's not to wake up the ol' folks. The ground is frozen hard; we stub our toes on the frozen ruts in the road. When we come to the minister's house, Laura is standin' on the front stoop, a-waitin' for us. Laura is the minister's daughter. She's a friend o' Sister Helen's— pretty as a dagerr'otype, an' gentle-like and tender. Laura lets me carry her skates, an' I'm glad of it, although I have my hands full already with the lantern, the hockies, and the rest. Hiram Peabody keeps us waitin', for he has overslept himself, an' when he comes trottin' out at last the girls make fun of him,—all except Sister Mary, an' she sort o' sticks up for Hiram, an' we're all so 'cute we kind o' calc'late we know the reason why.

"And now," said Ezra, softly, "the pictur' changes; seems as if I could see the pond. The ice is like a black lookin'-glass, and Hiram Peabody slips up the first thing, an' down he comes lickety-split, an' we all laugh,—except Sister Mary, an' she says it is very imp'lite to laugh at other folks' misfortunes. Ough! how cold it is, and how my fingers ache with the frost when I take off my mittens to strap on Laura's skates! But, oh, how my cheeks burn! And how careful I am not to hurt Laura, an' how I ask her if that's 'tight enough,' an' how she tells me 'jist a little tighter,' and how we two keep foolin' along till the others hev gone an' we are left alone! An' how quick I get my own skates strapped on,—none o' your new-fangled skates with springs an' plates an' clamps an' such, but honest, ol'- fashioned wooden ones with steel runners that curl up over my toes an' have a bright brass button on the end! How I strap 'em and lash 'em and buckle 'em on! An' Laura waits for me an' tells me to be sure to get 'em on tight enough,—why, bless me! after I once got 'em strapped on, if them skates hed come off, the feet wud ha' come with 'em! An' now away we go,—Laura an' me. Around the bend—near the medder where Si Barker's dog killed a woodchuck last summer—we meet the rest. We forget all about the cold. We run races an' play snap the whip, an' cut all sorts o' didoes, an' we never mind the pick'rel weed that is froze in on the ice an' trips us up every time we cut the outside edge; an' then we boys jump over the air-holes, an' the girls stan' by an' scream an' tell us they know we're agoin' to drown ourselves. So the hours go, an' it is sun-up at last, an' Sister Helen says we must be gettin' home. When we take our skates off, our feet feel as if they were wood. Laura has lost her tippet; I lend her mine, and she kind o' blushes. The old pond seems glad to have us go, and the fire-hangbird's nest in the willer-tree waves us good-by. Laura promises to come over to our house in the evenin', and so we break up.

"Seems now," continued Ezra, musingly,—"seems now as if I could see us all at breakfast. The race on the pond has made us hungry, and Mother says she never knew anybody else's boys that had such capac'ties as hers. It is the Yankee Thanksgivin' breakfast,—sausages an' fried potatoes, an' buckwheat cakes an' syrup,—maple syrup, mind ye, for Father has his own sugar bush, and there was a big run o' sap last season. Mother says, 'Ezry an' Amos, won't you never get through eatin'? We want to clear off the table, for there's pies to make, an' nuts to crack, and laws sakes alive! the turkey's got to be stuffed yit!' Then how we all fly round! Mother sends Helen up into the attic to get a squash while Mary's makin' the pie-crust. Amos an' I crack the walnuts,—they call 'em hickory nuts out in this pesky country of sagebrush and pasture land. The walnuts are hard, and it's all we can do to crack 'em. Ev'ry once'n a while one on 'em slips outer our fingers an' goes dancin' over the floor or flies into the pan Helen is squeezin' pumpkin into through the col'nder. Helen says we're shif'less an' good for nothin' but frivolin'; but Mother tells us how to crack the walnuts so's not to let 'em fly all over the room, an' so's not to be all jammed to pieces like the walnuts was down at the party at the Peasleys' last winter. An' now here comes Tryphena Foster, with her gingham gown an' muslin apron on; her folks have gone up to Amherst for Thanksgivin', an' Tryphena has come over to help our folks get dinner. She thinks a great deal o' Mother, 'cause Mother teaches her Sunday-school class an' says Tryphena oughter marry a missionary. There is bustle everywhere, the rattle uv pans an' the clatter of dishes; an' the new kitch'n stove begins to warm up an' git red, till Helen loses her wits an' is flustered, an' sez she never could git the hang o' that stove's dampers.

"An' now," murmured Ezra, gently, as a tone of deeper reverence crept into his voice, "I can see Father sittin' all by himself in the parlor. Father's hair is very gray, and there are wrinkles on his honest old face. He is lookin' through the winder at the Holyoke hills over yonder, and I can guess he's thinkin' of the time when he wuz a boy like me an' Amos, an' useter climb over them hills an' kill rattlesnakes an' hunt partridges. Or doesn't his eyes quite reach the Holyoke hills? Do they fall kind o' lovingly but sadly on the little buryin' ground jest beyond the village? Ah, Father knows that spot, an' he loves it, too, for there are treasures there whose memory he wouldn't swap for all the world could give. So, while there is a kind o' mist in Father's eyes, I can see he is dreamin'-like of sweet an' tender things, and a-communin' with memory,—hearin' voices I never heard an' feelin' the tech of hands I never pressed; an' seein' Father's peaceful face I find it hard to think of a Thanksgivin' sweeter than Father's is.

"The pictur' in the firelight changes now," said Ezra, "an' seems as if I wuz in the old frame meetin'-house. The meetin'-house is on the hill, and meetin' begins at half pas' ten. Our pew is well up in front,—seems as if I could see it now. It has a long red cushion on the seat, and in the hymn-book rack there is a Bible an' a couple of Psalmodies. We walk up the aisle slow, and Mother goes in first; then comes Mary, then me, then Helen, then Amos, and then Father. Father thinks it is jest as well to have one o' the girls set in between me an' Amos. The meetin'-house is full, for everybody goes to meetin' Thanksgivin' day. The minister reads the proclamation an' makes a prayer, an' then he gives out a psalm, an' we all stan' up an' turn 'round an' join the choir. Sam Merritt has come up from Palmer to spend Thanksgivin' with the ol' folks, an' he is singin' tenor to-day in his ol' place in the choir. Some folks say he sings wonderful well, but I don't like Sam's voice. Laura sings soprano in the choir, and Sam stands next to her an' holds the book.

"Seems as if I could hear the minister's voice, full of earnestness an' melody, comin' from way up in his little round pulpit. He is tellin' us why we should be thankful, an', as he quotes Scriptur' an' Dr. Watts, we boys wonder how anybody can remember so much of the Bible. Then I get nervous and worried. Seems to me the minister was never comin' to lastly, and I find myself wonderin' whether Laura is listenin' to what the preachin' is about, or is writin' notes to Sam Merritt in the back of the tune book. I get thirsty, too, and I fidget about till Father looks at me, and Mother nudges Helen, and Helen passes it along to me with interest.

"An' then," continues Ezra in his revery, "when the last hymn is given out an' we stan' up agin an' join the choir, I am glad to see that Laura is singin' outer the book with Miss Hubbard, the alto. An' goin' out o' meetin' I kind of edge up to Laura and ask her if I kin have the pleasure of seein' her home.

"An' now we boys all go out on the Common to play ball. The Enfield boys have come over, and, as all the Hampshire county folks know, they are tough fellers to beat. Gorham Polly keeps tally, because he has got the newest jack-knife,—oh, how slick it whittles the old broom-handle Gorham picked up in Packard's store an' brought along jest to keep tally on! It is a great game of ball; the bats are broad and light, and the ball is small and soft. But the Enfield boys beat us at last; leastwise they make 70 tallies to our 58, when Heman Fitts knocks the ball over into Aunt Dorcas Eastman's yard, and Aunt Dorcas comes out an' picks up the ball an' takes it into the house, an' we have to stop playin'. Then Phineas Owens allows he can flop any boy in Belchertown, an' Moses Baker takes him up, an' they wrassle like two tartars, till at last Moses tuckers Phineas out an' downs him as slick as a whistle.

"Then we all go home, for Thanksgivin' dinner is ready. Two long tables have been made into one, and one of the big tablecloths Gran'ma had when she set up housekeepin' is spread over 'em both. We all set round,—Father, Mother, Aunt Lydia Holbrook, Uncle Jason, Mary, Helen, Tryphena Foster, Amos, and me. How big an' brown the turkey is, and how good it smells! There are bounteous dishes of mashed potato, turnip, an' squash, and the celery is very white and cold, the biscuits are light an' hot, and the stewed cranberries are red as Laura's cheeks. Amos and I get the drumsticks; Mary wants the wish-bone to put over the door for Hiram, but Helen gets it. Poor Mary, she always did have to give up to 'rushin' Helen,' as we call her. The pies,—oh, what pies mother makes; no dyspepsia in 'em, but good-nature an' good health an' hospitality! Pumpkin pies, mince an' apple too, and then a big dish of pippins an' russets an' bellflowers, an', last of all, walnuts with cider from the Zebrina Dickerson farm! I tell ye, there's a Thanksgivin' dinner for ye! that's what we get in old Belchertown; an' that's the kind of livin' that makes the Yankees so all-fired good an' smart.

"But the best of all," said Ezra, very softly to himself,—"oh, yes, the best scene in all the pictur' is when evenin' comes, when the lamps are lit in the parlor, when the neighbors come in, and when there is music an' singin' an' games. An' it's this part o' the pictur' that makes me homesick now and fills my heart with a longin' I never had before; an' yet it sort o' mellows an' comforts me, too. Miss Serena Cadwell, whose beau was killed in the war, plays on the melodeon, and we all sing,—all on us, men, womenfolks, an' children. Sam Merritt is there, an' he sings a tenor song about love. The women sort of whisper round that he's goin' to be married to a Palmer lady nex' spring, an' I think to myself I never heard better singin' than Sam's. Then we play games,—proverbs, buzz, clap-in-clap-out, copenhagen, fox-an'-geese, button-button-who's-got-the-button, spin-the-platter, go-to-

Jerusalem, my-ship's-come-in, and all the rest. The ol' folks play with the young folks just as nat'ral as can be; and we all laugh when Deacon Hosea Cowles hez to measure six yards of love ribbon with Miss Hepsy Newton, and cut each yard with a kiss; for the deacon hez been sort o' purrin' round Miss Hepsy for goin' on two years. Then, aft'r a while, when Mary an' Helen bring in the cookies, nutcakes, cider, an' apples, Mother says: 'I don't b'lieve we're goin' to hev enough apples to go round; Ezry, I guess I'll have to get you to go down-cellar for some more.' Then I says: 'All right, Mother, I'll go, providin' some one'll go along an' hold the candle.' An' when I say this I look right at Laura, an' she blushes. Then Helen, jest for meanness, says: 'Ezry, I s'pose you aint willin' to have your fav'rite sister go down-cellar with you an' catch her death o' cold?' But Mary, who hez been showin' Hiram Peabody the phot'graph album for more 'n an hour, comes to the rescue an' makes Laura take the candle, and she shows Laura how to hold it so it won't go out.

"The cellar is warm an' dark. There are cobwebs all between the rafters an' everywhere else except on the shelves where Mother keeps the butter an' eggs an' other things that would freeze in the butt'ry upstairs. The apples are in bar'ls up against the wall, near the potater-bin. How fresh an' sweet they smell! Laura thinks she sees a mouse, an' she trembles an' wants to jump up on the pork bar'l, but I tell her that there sha'n't no mouse hurt her while I'm round; and I mean it, too, for the sight of Laura a-tremblin' makes me as strong as one of Father's steers. 'What kind of apples do you like best, Ezry?' asks Laura,—'russets or greenin's or crow-eggs or bellflowers or Baldwins or pippins?' 'I like the Baldwins best,' says I, "coz they've got red cheeks just like yours.' 'Why, Ezry Thompson! how you talk!' says Laura. 'You oughter be ashamed of yourself!' But when I get the dish filled up with apples there aint a Baldwin in all the lot that can compare with the bright red of Laura's cheeks. An' Laura knows it, too, an' she sees the mouse agin, an' screams, and then the candle goes out, and we are in a dreadful stew. But I, bein' almost a man, contrive to bear up under it, and knowin' she is an orph'n, I comfort an' encourage Laura the best I know how, and we are almost upstairs when Mother comes to the door and wants to know what has kep' us so long. Jest as if Mother doesn't know! Of course she does; an' when Mother kisses Laura good-by that night there is in the act a tenderness that speaks more sweetly than even Mother's words.

"It is so like Mother," mused Ezra; "so like her with her gentleness an' clingin' love. Hers is the sweetest picture of all, and hers the best love."

Dream on, Ezra; dream of the old home with its dear ones, its holy influences, and its precious inspiration,—mother. Dream on in the far-away firelight; and as the angel hand of memory unfolds these sacred visions, with thee and them shall abide, like a Divine comforter, the spirit of thanksgiving.

CHAPTER XIV

LUDWIG AND ELOISE

Once upon a time there were two youths named Herman and Ludwig; and they both loved Eloise, the daughter of the old burgomaster. Now, the old burgomaster was very rich, and having no child but Eloise, he was anxious that she should be well married and settled in life. "For," said he, "death is likely to come to me at any time: I am old and feeble, and I want to see my child sheltered by another's love before I am done with earth forever."

Eloise was much beloved by all the youth in the village, and there was not one who would not gladly have taken her to wife; but none loved her so much as did Herman and Ludwig. Nor did Eloise care for any but Herman and Ludwig, and she loved Herman. The burgomaster said: "Choose whom you will—I care not! So long as he be honest I will have him for a son and thank Heaven for him."

So Eloise chose Herman, and all said she chose wisely; for Herman was young and handsome, and by his valor had won distinction in the army, and had thrice been complimented by the general. So when the brave young captain led Eloise to the altar there was great rejoicing in the village. The beaux, forgetting their disappointments, and the maidens, seeing the cause of all their jealousy removed, made merry together; and it was said that never had there been in the history of the province an event so joyous as was the wedding of Herman and Eloise.

But in all the Village there was one aching heart. Ludwig, the young musician, saw with quiet despair the maiden he loved go to the altar with another. He had known Eloise from childhood, and he could not say when his love of her began, it was so very long ago; but now he knew his heart was consumed by a hopeless passion. Once, at a village festival, he had begun to speak to her of his love; but Eloise had placed her hand kindly upon his lips and told him to say no further, for they had always been and always would be brother and sister. So Ludwig never spoke his love after that, and Eloise and he were as brother and sister; but the love of her grew always within him, and he had no thought but of her.

And now, when Eloise and Herman were wed, Ludwig feigned that he had received a message from a rich relative in a distant part of the kingdom bidding him come thither, and Ludwig went from the village and was seen there no more.

When the burgomaster died all his possessions went to Herman and Eloise; and they were accounted the richest folk in the province, and so good and charitable were they that they were beloved by all. Meanwhile Herman had risen to greatness in the army, for by his valorous exploits he had become a general, and he was much endeared to the king. And Eloise and Herman lived in a great castle in the midst of a beautiful park, and the people came and paid them reverence there.

And no one in all these years spoke of Ludwig. No one thought of him. Ludwig was forgotten. And so the years went by.

It came to pass, however, that from a far-distant province there spread the fame of a musician so great that the king sent for him to visit the court. No one knew the musician's name nor whence he came, for he lived alone and would never speak of himself; but his music was so tender and beautiful that it was called heart-music, and he himself was called the Master. He was old and bowed with infirmities, but his music was always of youth and love; it touched every heart with its simplicity and pathos, and all wondered how this old and broken man could create so much of tenderness and sweetness on these themes.

But when the king sent for the Master to come to court the Master returned him answer: "No, I am old and feeble. To leave my home would weary me unto death. Let me die here as I have lived these long years, weaving my music for hearts that need my solace."

Then the people wondered. But the king was not angry; in pity he sent the Master a purse of gold, and bade him come or not come, as he willed. Such honor had never before been shown any subject in the kingdom, and all the people were dumb with amazement. But the Master gave the purse of gold to the poor of the village wherein he lived.

In those days Herman died, full of honors and years, and there was a great lamentation in the land, for Herman was beloved by all. And Eloise wept unceasingly and would not be comforted.

On the seventh day after Herman had been buried there came to the castle in the park an aged and bowed man who carried in his white and trembling hands a violin. His kindly face was deeply wrinkled, and a venerable beard swept down upon his breast. He was weary and footsore, but he heeded not the words of pity bestowed on him by all who beheld him tottering on his way. He knocked boldly at the castle gate, and demanded to be brought into the presence of Eloise.

And Eloise said: "Bid him enter; perchance his music will comfort my breaking heart."

Then, when the old man had come into her presence, behold! he was the Master,—ay, the Master whose fame was in every land, whose heart-music was on every tongue.

"If thou art indeed the Master," said Eloise, "let thy music be balm to my chastened spirit."

The Master said: "Ay, Eloise, I will comfort thee in thy sorrow, and thy heart shall be stayed, and a great joy will come to thee."

Then the Master drew his bow across the strings, and lo! forthwith there arose such harmonies as Eloise had never heard before. Gently, persuasively, they stole upon her senses and filled her soul with an ecstasy of peace.

"Is it Herman that speaks to me?" cried Eloise. "It is his voice I hear, and it speaks to me of love. With thy heart-music, O Master, all the sweetness of his life comes back to comfort me!"

The Master did not pause; as he played, it seemed as if each tender word and caress of Herman's life was stealing back on music's pinions to soothe the wounds that death had made.

"It is the song of our love-life," murmured Eloise. "How full of memories it is—what tenderness and harmony—and, oh! what peace it brings! But tell me, Master, what means this minor chord,—this undertone of sadness and of pathos that flows like a deep, unfathomable current throughout it all, and wailing, weaves itself about thy theme of love and happiness with its weird and subtile influences?"

Then the Master said: "It is that shade of sorrow and sacrifice, O Eloise, that ever makes the picture of love more glorious. An undertone of pathos has been my part in all these years to symmetrize the love of Herman and Eloise. The song of thy love is beautiful, and who shall say it is not beautified by the sad undertone of Ludwig's broken heart?"

"Thou art Ludwig!" cried Eloise. "Thou art Ludwig, who didst love me, and hast come to comfort me who loved thee not!"

The Master indeed was Ludwig; but when they hastened to do him homage he heard them not, for with that last and sweetest heart-song his head sank upon his breast, and he was dead.

CHAPTER XV

FIDO'S LITTLE FRIEND

One morning in May Fido sat on the front porch, and he was deep in thought. He was wondering whether the people who were moving into the next house were as cross and unfeeling as the people who had just moved out. He hoped they were not, for the people who had just moved out had never treated Fido with that respect and kindness which Fido believed he was on all occasions entitled to.

"The new-comers must be nice folks," said Fido to himself, "for their feather-beds look big and comfortable, and their baskets are all ample and generous,—and see, there goes a bright gilt cage, and there is a plump yellow canary bird in it! Oh, how glad Mrs. Tabby will be to see it,—she so dotes on dear little canary birds!"

Mrs. Tabby was the old brindled cat, who was the mother of the four cunning little kittens in the hay-mow. Fido had heard her remark very purringly only a few days ago that she longed for a canary bird, just to amuse her little ones and give them correct musical ears. Honest old Fido! There was no guile in his heart, and he never dreamed there was in all the wide world such a sin as hypocrisy. So when Fido saw the little canary bird in the cage he was glad for Mrs. Tabby's sake.

While Fido sat on the front porch and watched the people moving into the next house another pair of eyes peeped out of the old hollow maple over the way. This was the red-headed woodpecker, who had a warm, cosey nest far down in the old hollow maple, and in the nest there were four beautiful eggs, of which the red-headed woodpecker was very proud.

"Good-morning, Mr. Fido," called the red-headed woodpecker from her high perch. "You are out bright and early to-day. And what do you think of our new neighbors?"

"Upon my word, I cannot tell," replied Fido, wagging his tail cheerily, "for I am not acquainted with them. But I have been watching them closely, and by to-day noon I think I shall be on speaking terms with them,—provided, of course, they are not the cross, unkind people our old neighbors were."

"Oh, I do so hope there are no little boys in the family," sighed the red-headed woodpecker; and then she added, with much determination and a defiant toss of her beautiful head: "I hate little boys!"

"Why so?" inquired Fido. "As for myself, I love little boys. I have always found them the pleasantest of companions. Why do you dislike them?"

"Because they are wicked," said the red-headed woodpecker. "They climb trees and break up the nests we have worked so hard to build, and they steal away our lovely eggs—oh, I hate little boys!"

"Good little boys don't steal birds' eggs," said Fido, "and I'm sure I never would play with a bad boy."

But the red-headed woodpecker insisted that all little boys were wicked; and, firm in this faith, she flew away to the linden over yonder, where, she had heard the thrush say, there lived a family of fat white grubs. The red-headed woodpecker wanted her breakfast, and it would have been hard to find a more palatable morsel for her than a white fat grub.

As for Fido, he sat on the front porch and watched the people moving in. And as he watched them he thought of what the red-headed woodpecker had said, and he wondered whether it could be possible for little boys to be so cruel as to rob birds' nests. As he brooded over this sad possibility, his train of thought was interrupted by the sound of a voice that fell pleasantly on his ears.

"Goggie, goggie, goggie!" said the voice. "Tum here, 'ittle goggie—tum here, goggie, goggie, goggie!"

Fido looked whence the voice seemed to come, and he saw a tiny figure on the other side of the fence,—a cunning baby-figure in the yard that belonged to the house where the new neighbors were moving in. A second glance assured Fido that the calling stranger was a little boy not more than three years old, wearing a pretty dress, and a broad hat that crowned his yellow hair and shaded his big blue eyes and dimpled face. The sight was a pleasing one, and Fido vibrated his tail,—very cautiously, however, for Fido was not quite certain that the little boy meant his greeting for him, and Fido's sad experiences with the old neighbors had made him wary about scraping acquaintances too hastily.

"Tum, 'ittle goggie!" persisted the prattling stranger, and, as if to encourage Fido, the little boy stretched his chubby arms through the fence and waved them entreatingly.

Fido was convinced now; so he got up, and with many cordial gestures of his hospitable tail, trotted down the steps and over the lawn to the corner of the fence where the little stranger was.

"Me love oo," said the little stranger, patting Fido's honest brown back; "me love oo, 'ittle goggie."

Fido knew that, for there were caresses in every stroke of the dimpled hands. Fido loved the little boy, too,—yes, all at once he loved the little boy; and he licked the dimpled hands, and gave three short, quick barks, and wagged his tail hysterically. So then and there began the friendship of Fido and the little boy.

Presently Fido crawled under the fence into the next yard, and then the little boy sat down on the grass, and Fido put his forepaws in the little boy's lap and cocked up his ears and looked up into the little boy's face, as much as to say, "We shall be great friends, shall we not, little boy?"

"Me love oo," said the little boy; "me wan' to tiss oo, 'ittle goggie!"

And the little boy did kiss Fido,—yes, right on Fido's cold nose; and Fido liked to have the little boy kiss him, for it reminded him of another little boy who used to kiss him, but who was now so big that he was almost ashamed to play with Fido any more.

"Is oo sit, 'ittle goggie?" asked the little boy, opening his blue eyes to their utmost capacity and looking very piteous. "Oo nose be so told, oo mus' be sit, 'ittle goggie!"

But no, Fido was not sick, even though his nose was cold. Oh, no; he romped and played all that morning in the cool, green grass with the little boy; and the red-headed woodpecker, clinging to the bark on the hickory-tree, laughed at their merry antics till her sides ached and her beautiful head turned fairly livid. Then, at last, the little boy's mamma came out of the house and told him he had played long enough; and neither the red-headed woodpecker nor Fido saw him again that day.

But the next morning the little boy toddled down to the fence-corner, bright and early, and called, "Goggie! goggie! goggie!" so loudly, that Fido heard him in the wood-shed, where he was holding a morning chat with Mrs. Tabby. Fido hastened to answer the call; the way he spun out of the wood-shed and down the gravel walk and around the corner of the house was a marvel.

"Mamma says oo dot f'eas, 'ittle goggie," said the little boy. "Has oo dot f'eas?"

Fido looked crestfallen, for could Fido have spoken he would have confessed that he indeed was afflicted with fleas,—not with very many fleas, but just enough to interrupt his slumbers and his meditations at the most inopportune moments. And the little boy's guileless impeachment set Fido to feeling creepy-crawly all of a sudden, and without any further ado Fido turned deftly in his tracks, twisted his head back toward his tail, and by means of several well-directed bites and plunges gave the malicious Bedouins thereabouts located timely warning to behave themselves. The little boy thought this performance very funny, and he laughed heartily. But Fido looked crestfallen.

Oh, what play and happiness they had that day; how the green grass kissed their feet, and how the smell of clover came with the springtime breezes from the meadow yonder! The red-headed woodpecker heard them at play, and she clambered out of the hollow maple and dodged hither and thither as if she, too, shared their merriment. Yes, and the yellow thistle-bird, whose nest was in the blooming lilac-bush, came and perched in the pear-tree and sang a little song about the dear little eggs in her cunning home. And there was a flower in the fence-corner,—a sweet, modest flower that no human eyes but the little boy's had ever seen,—and she sang a little song, too, a song about the kind old mother earth and the pretty sunbeams, the gentle rain and the droning bees. Why, the little boy had never known anything half so beautiful, and Fido,—he, too, was delighted beyond all telling. If the whole truth must be told, Fido had such an exciting and bewildering romp that day that when night came, and he lay asleep on the kitchen floor, he dreamed he was tumbling in the green grass with the little boy, and he tossed and barked and whined so in his sleep that the hired man had to get up in the night and put him out of doors.

Down in the pasture at the end of the lane lived an old woodchuck. Last year the freshet had driven him from his childhood's home in the cornfield by the brook, and now he resided in a snug hole in the pasture. During their rambles one day, Fido and his little boy friend had come to the pasture, and found the old woodchuck sitting upright at the entrance to his hole.

"Oh, I'm not going to hurt you, old Mr. Woodchuck," said Fido. "I have too much respect for your gray hairs."

"Thank you," replied the woodchuck, sarcastically, "but I'm not afraid of any bench-legged fyste that ever walked. It was only last week that I whipped Deacon Skinner's yellow mastiff, and I calc'late I can trounce you, you ridiculous little brown cur!"

The little boy did not hear this badinage. When he saw the woodchuck solemnly perched at the entrance to his hole he was simply delighted.

"Oh, see!" cried the little boy, stretching out his fat arms and running toward the woodchuck,—"oh, see,—nuzzer 'ittle goggie! Tum here, 'ittle goggie,—me love oo!"

But the old woodchuck was a shy creature, and not knowing what guile the little boy's cordial greeting might mask, the old woodchuck discreetly disappeared in his hole, much to the little boy's amazement.

Nevertheless, the old woodchuck, the little boy, and Fido became fast friends in time, and almost every day they visited together in the pasture. The old woodchuck—hoary and scarred veteran that he was—had wonderful stories to tell,—stories of marvellous adventures, of narrow escapes, of battles with cruel dogs, and of thrilling experiences that were altogether new to his wondering listeners. Meanwhile the red-headed woodpecker's eggs in the hollow maple had hatched, and the proud mother had great tales to tell of her baby birds,—of how beautiful and knowing they were, and of what good, noble birds they were going to be when they grew up. The yellow-bird, too, had four fuzzy little babies in her nest in the lilac-bush, and every now and then she came to sing to the little boy and Fido of her darlings. Then, when the little boy and Fido were tired with play, they would sit in the rowen near the fence-corner and hear the flower tell a story the dew had brought fresh from the stars the night before. They all loved each other,—the little boy, Fido, the old woodchuck, the red-headed woodpecker, the yellow-bird, and the flower,—yes, all through the days of spring and all through the summer time they loved each other in their own honest, sweet, simple way.

But one morning Fido sat on the front porch and wondered why the little boy had not come to the fence-corner and called to him. The sun was high, the men had been long gone to the harvest fields, and the heat of the early autumn day had driven the birds to the thickest foliage of the trees. Fido could not understand why the little boy did not come; he felt, oh! so lonesome, and he yearned for the sound of a little voice calling "Goggie, goggie, goggie."

The red-headed woodpecker could not explain it, nor could the yellow-bird. Fido trotted leisurely down to the fence-corner and asked the flower if she had seen the little boy that morning. But no, the flower had not laid eyes on the little boy, and she could only shake her head doubtfully when Fido asked her what it all meant. At last in desperation Fido braced himself for an heroic solution of the mystery, and as loudly as ever he could, he barked three times,—in the hope, you know, that the little boy would hear his call and come. But the little boy did not come.

Then Fido trotted sadly down the lane to the pasture to talk with the old woodchuck about this strange thing. The old woodchuck saw him coming and ambled out to meet him.

"But where is our little boy?" asked the old woodchuck.

"I do not know," said Fido. "I waited for him and called to him again and again, but he never came."

Ah, those were sorry days for the little boy's friends, and sorriest for Fido. Poor, honest Fido, how lonesome he was and how he moped about! How each sudden sound, how each footfall, startled him! How he sat all those days upon the front door-stoop, with his eyes fixed on the fence-corner and his rough brown ears cocked up as if he expected each moment to see two chubby arms stretched out toward him and to hear a baby voice calling "Goggie, goggie, goggie."

Once only they saw him,—Fido, the flower, and the others. It was one day when Fido had called louder than usual. They saw a little figure in a night-dress come to an upper window and lean his arms out. They saw it was the little boy, and, oh! how pale and ill he looked. But his yellow hair was as glorious as ever, and the dimples came back with the smile that lighted his thin little face when he saw Fido; and he leaned on the window casement and waved his baby hands feebly, and cried: "Goggie! goggie!" till Fido saw the little boy's mother come and take him from the window.

One morning Fido came to the fence-corner—how very lonely that spot seemed now—and he talked with the flower and the woodpecker; and the yellow-bird came, too, and they all talked of the little boy. And at that very moment the old woodchuck reared his hoary head by the hole in the pasture, and he looked this way and that and wondered why the little boy never came any more.

"Suppose," said Fido to the yellow-bird,—"suppose you fly to the window way up there and see what the little boy is doing. Sing him one of your pretty songs, and tell him we are lonesome without him; that we are waiting for him in the old fence-corner."

Then the yellow-bird did as Fido asked,—she flew to the window where they had once seen the little boy, and alighting upon the sill, she peered into the room. In another moment she was back on the bush at Fido's side.

"He is asleep," said the yellow-bird.

"Asleep!" cried Fido.

"Yes," said the yellow-bird, "he is fast asleep. I think he must be dreaming a beautiful dream, for I could see a smile on his face, and his little hands were folded on his bosom. There were flowers all about him, and but for their sweet voices the chamber would have been very still."

"Come, let us wake him," said Fido; "let us all call to him at once. Then perhaps he will hear us and awaken and answer; perhaps he will come."

So they all called in chorus,—Fido and the other honest friends. They called so loudly that the still air of that autumn morning was strangely startled, and the old woodchuck in the pasture way off yonder heard the echoes and wondered.

"Little boy! little boy!" they called, "why are you sleeping? Why are you sleeping, little boy?"

Call on, dear voices! but the little boy will never hear. The dimpled hands that caressed you are indeed folded upon his breast; the lips that kissed your honest faces are sealed; the baby voice that sang your playtime songs with you is hushed, and all about him is the fragrance and the beauty of flowers. Call on, O honest friends! but he shall never hear your calling; for, as if he were aweary of the love and play and sunshine that were all he knew of earth, our darling is asleep forever.

CHAPTER XVI

THE OLD MAN

I called him the Old Man, but he wuzn't an old man; he wuz a little boy—our fust one; 'nd his gran'ma, who'd had a heap of experience in sich matters, allowed that he wuz for looks as likely a child as she'd ever clapped eyes on. Bein' our fust, we sot our hearts on him, and Lizzie named him Willie, for that wuz the name she liked best, havin' had a brother Willyum killed in the war. But I never called him anything but the Old Man, and that name seemed to fit him, for he wuz one of your sollum babies,—alwuz thinkin' 'nd thinkin' 'nd thinkin', like he wuz a jedge, and when he laffed it wuzn't like other children's laffs, it wuz so sad-like.

Lizzie 'nd I made it up between us that when the Old Man growed up we'd send him to collige 'nd give him a lib'ril edication, no matter though we had to sell the farm to do it. But we never cud exactly agree as to what we was goin' to make of him; Lizzie havin' her heart sot on his bein' a preacher like his gran'pa Baker, and I wantin' him to be a lawyer 'nd git rich out'n the corporations, like his uncle Wilson Barlow. So we never come to no definite conclusion as to what the Old Man wuz goin' to be bime by; but while we wuz thinkin' 'nd debatin' the Old Man kep' growin' 'nd growin', and all the time he wuz as serious 'nd sollum as a jedge.

Lizzie got jest wrapt up in that boy; toted him round ever'where 'nd never let on like it made her tired,—powerful big 'nd hearty child too, but heft warn't nothin' 'longside of Lizzie's love for the Old Man. When he caught the measles from Sairy Baxter's baby Lizzie sot up day 'nd night till he wuz well, holdin' his hands 'nd singin' songs to him, 'nd cryin' herse'f almost to death because she dassent give him cold water to drink when he called f'r it. As for me, my heart wuz wrapt up in the

Old Man, too, but, bein' a man, it wuzn't for me to show it like Lizzie, bein' a woman; and now that the Old Man is—wall, now that he has gone, it wouldn't do to let on how much I sot by him, for that would make Lizzie feel all the wuss.

Sometimes, when I think of it, it makes me sorry that I didn't show the Old Man some way how much I wuz wrapt up in him. Used to hold him in my lap 'nd make faces for him 'nd alder whistles 'nd things; sometimes I'd kiss him on his rosy cheek, when nobody wuz lookin'; onct I tried to sing him a song, but it made him cry, 'nd I never tried my hand at singin' again. But, somehow, the Old Man didn't take to me like he took to his mother: would climb down outern my lap to git where Lizzie wuz; would hang on to her gownd, no matter what she wuz doin',—whether she was makin' bread, or sewin', or puttin' up pickles, it wuz alwuz the same to the Old Man; he wuzn't happy unless he wuz right there, clost beside his mother.

Most all boys, as I've heern tell, is proud to be round with their father, doin' what he does 'nd wearin' the kind of clothes he wears. But the Old Man wuz diff'rent; he allowed that his mother wuz his best friend, 'nd the way he stuck to her—wall, it has alwuz been a great comfort to Lizzie to recollect it.

The Old Man had a kind of confidin' way with his mother. Every oncet in a while, when he'd be playin' by hisself in the front room, he'd call out, "Mudder, mudder;" and no matter where Lizzie wuz,—in the kitchen, or in the wood-shed, or in the yard, she'd answer: "What is it, darlin'?" Then the Old Man 'ud say: "Tum here, mudder, I wanter tell you sumfin'." Never could find out what the Old Man wanted to tell Lizzie; like 's not he didn't wanter tell her nothin'; may be he wuz lonesome 'nd jest wanted to feel that Lizzie wuz round. But that didn't make no diff'rence; it wuz all the same to Lizzie. No matter where she wuz or what she wuz a-doin', jest as soon as the Old Man told her he wanted to tell her somethin' she dropped ever'thing else 'nd went straight to him. Then the Old Man would laff one of his sollum, sad-like laffs, 'nd put his arms round Lizzie's neck 'nd whisper—or pertend to whisper—somethin' in her ear, 'nd Lizzie would laff 'nd say, "Oh, what a nice secret we have atween us!" and then she would kiss the Old Man 'nd go back to her work.

Time changes all things,—all things but memory, nothin' can change that. Seems like it wuz only yesterday or the day before that I heern the Old Man callin', "Mudder, mudder, I wanter tell you sumfin'," and that I seen him put his arms around her neck 'nd whisper softly to her.

It had been an open winter, 'nd there wuz fever all around us. The Baxters lost their little girl, and Homer Thompson's children had all been taken down. Ev'ry night 'nd mornin' we prayed God to save our darlin'; but one evenin' when I come up from the wood lot, the Old Man wuz restless 'nd his face wuz hot 'nd he talked in his sleep. May be you've been through it yourself,—may be you've tended a child that's down with the fever; if so, may be you know what we went through, Lizzie 'nd me. The doctor shook his head one night when he come to see the Old Man; we knew what that meant. I went out-doors,—I couldn't stand it in the room there, with the Old Man seein' 'nd talkin' about things that the fever made him see. I wuz too big a coward to stay 'nd help his mother to bear up; so I went out-doors 'nd brung in wood,—brung in wood enough to last all spring,—and then I sat down alone by the kitchen fire 'nd heard the clock tick 'nd watched the shadders flicker through the room.

I remember Lizzie's comin' to me and sayin': "He's breathin' strange-like, 'nd has little feet is cold as ice." Then I went into the front chamber where he lay. The day wuz breakin'; the cattle wuz lowin' outside; a beam of light come through the winder and fell on the Old Man's face,—perhaps it wuz the summons for which he waited and which shall some time come to me 'nd you. Leastwise the Old Man roused from his sleep 'nd opened up his big blue eyes. It wuzn't me he wanted to see.

"Mudder! mudder!" cried the Old Man, but his voice warn't strong 'nd clear like it used to be. "Mudder, where be you, mudder?"

Then, breshin' by me, Lizzie caught the Old Man up 'nd held him in her arms, like she had done a thousand times before.

"What is it, darlin'? Here I be," says Lizzie.

"Tum here," says the Old Man,—"tum here; I wanter tell you sumfin'."

The Old Man went to reach his arms around her neck 'nd whisper in her ear. But his arms fell limp and helpless-like, 'nd the Old Man's curly head drooped on his mother's breast.

CHAPTER XVII

BILL, THE LOKIL EDITOR

Bill wuz alluz fond uv children 'nd birds 'nd flowers. Aint it kind o' curious how sometimes we find a great, big, awkward man who loves sech things? Bill had the biggest feet in the township, but I'll bet my wallet that he never trod on a violet in all his life. Bill never took no slack from enny man that wuz sober, but the children made him play with 'em, and he'd set for hours a-watchin' the yaller-hammer buildin' her nest in the old cottonwood.

Now I aint defendin' Bill; I'm jest tellin' the truth about him. Nothink I kin say one way or t'other is goin' to make enny difference now; Bill's dead 'nd buried, 'nd the folks is discussin' him 'nd wond'rin' whether his immortal soul is all right. Sometimes I hev worried 'bout Bill, but I don't worry 'bout him no more. Uv course Bill had his faults,—I never liked that drinkin' business uv his'n, yet I allow that Bill got more good out'n likker, and likker got more good out'n Bill, than I ever see before or sence. It warn't when the likker wuz in Bill that Bill wuz at his best, but when he hed been on to one uv his bats 'nd had drunk himself sick 'nd wuz comin' out uv the other end of the bat, then Bill wuz one uv the meekest 'nd properest critters you ever seen. An' potry? Some uv the most beautiful potry I ever read wuz writ by Bill when he wuz recoverin' himself out'n one uv them bats. Seemed like it kind uv exalted an' purified Bill's nachur to git drunk an' git over it. Bill cud drink more likker 'nd be sorrier for it than any other man in seven States. There never wuz a more penitent feller than he wuz when he wuz soberin'. The trubble with Bill seemed to be that his conscience didn't come on watch quite of'n enuff.

It'll be ten years come nex' spring since Bill showed up here. I don't know whar he come from; seemed like he didn't want to talk about his past. I allers suspicioned that he had seen trubble— maybe, sorrer. I reecollect that one time he got a telegraph,—Mr. Ivins told me 'bout it afterwards,—and when he read it he put his hands up to his face 'nd groaned, like. That day he got full uv likker 'nd he kep' full of likker for a week; but when he come round all right he wrote a pome for the paper, 'nd the name of the pome wuz "Mary," but whether Mary wuz his sister or his wife or an old sweetheart uv his'n I never knew. But it looked from the pome like she wuz dead 'nd that he loved her.

Bill wuz the best lokil the paper ever had. He didn't hustle around much, but he had a kind er pleasin' way uv dishin' things up. He cud be mighty comical when he sot out to be, but his best holt was serious pieces. Nobody could beat Bill writin' obituaries. When old Mose Holbrook wuz dyin' the minister sez to him: "Mr. Holbrook, you seem to be sorry that you're passin' away to a better land?"

"Wall, no; not exactly that," sez Mose, "but to be frank with you, I hev jest one regret in connection with this affair."

"What's that?" asked the minister.

"I can't help feelin' sorry," sez Mose, "that I aint goin' to hev the pleasure uv readin' what Bill Newton sez about me in the paper. I know it'll be sumthin' uncommon fine; I loant him two dollars a year ago last fall."

The Higginses lost a darned good friend when Bill died. Bill wrote a pome 'bout their old dog Towze when he wuz run over by Watkins's hay wagon seven years ago. I'll bet that pome is in every scrap-book in the county. You couldn't read that pome without cryin',—why, that pome wud hev brought a dew out on the desert uv Sary. Old Tim Hubbard, the meanest man in the State, borrered a paper to read the pome, and he wuz so 'fected by it that he never borrered anuther paper as long as he lived. I don't more'n half reckon, though, that the Higginses appreciated what Bill had done for 'em. I never heerd uv their givin' him anythink more'n a basket uv greenin' apples, and Bill wrote a piece 'bout the apples nex' day.

But Bill wuz at his best when he wrote things about the children,—about the little ones that died, I mean. Seemed like Bill had a way of his own of sayin' things that wuz beautiful 'nd tender; he said he loved the children because they wuz innocent, and I reckon—yes, I know he did, for the pomes he writ about 'em showed he did.

When our little Alice died I started out for Mr. Miller's; he wuz the undertaker. The night wuz powerful dark, 'nd it wuz all the darker to me, because seemed like all the light hed gone out in my life. Down near the bridge I met Bill; he weaved round in the road, for he wuz in likker.

"Hello, Mr. Baker," sez he, "whar be you goin' this time o' night?"

"Bill," sez I, "I'm goin' on the saddest errand uv my life."

"What d'ye mean?" sez he, comin' up to me as straight as he cud.

"Why, Bill," sez I, "our little girl—my little girl—Allie, you know—she's dead."

I hoarsed up so I couldn't say much more. And Bill didn't say nothink at all; he jest reached me his hand, and he took my hand and seemed like in that grasp his heart spoke many words of comfort to mine. And nex' day he had a piece in the paper about our little girl; we cut it out and put it in the big Bible in the front room. Sometimes when we get to fussin', Martha goes 'nd gets that bit of paper 'nd reads it to me; then us two kind uv cry to ourselves, 'nd we make it up between us for the dead child's sake.

Well, you kin see how it wuz that so many uv us liked Bill; he had soothed our hearts,—there's nothin' like sympathy after all. Bill's potry hed heart in it; it didn't surprise you or scare you; it jest got down in under your vest, 'nd before you knew it you wuz all choked up. I know all about your fashionable potry and your famous potes,—Martha took Godey's for a year. Folks that live in the city can't write potry,—not the real, genuine article. To write potry, as I figure it, the heart must have somethin' to feed on; you can't get that somethin' whar there aint trees 'nd grass 'nd birds 'nd flowers. Bill loved these things, and he fed his heart on 'em, and that's why his potry wuz so much better than anybody else's.

I aint worryin' much about Bill now; I take it that everythink is for the best. When they told me that Bill died in a drunken fit I felt that his end oughter have come some other way,—he wuz too good a man for that. But maybe, after all, it was ordered for the best. Jist imagine Bill a-standin' up for jedgment; jist imagine that poor, sorrowful, shiverin' critter waitin' for his turn to come. Pictur', if you can, how full uv penitence he is, 'nd how full uv potry 'nd gentleness 'nd misery. The Lord aint agoin' to be too hard on that poor wretch. Of course we can't comprehend Divine mercy; we only know that it is full of compassion,—a compassion infinitely tenderer and sweeter than ours. And the more I think on 't, the more I reckon that Bill will plead to win that mercy, for, like as not, the little ones—my Allie with the rest—will run to him when they see him in his trubble and will hold his tremblin' hands 'nd twine their arms about him, and plead, with him, for compassion.

You've seen an old sycamore that the lightnin' has struck; the ivy has reached up its vines 'nd spread 'em all around it 'nd over it, coverin' its scars 'nd splintered branches with a velvet green 'nd fillin' the air with fragrance. You've seen this thing and you know that it is beautiful.

That's Bill, perhaps, as he stands up f'r jedgment,—a miserable, tremblin', 'nd unworthy thing, perhaps, but twined about, all over, with singin' and pleadin' little children—and that is pleasin' in God's sight, I know.

What would you—what would I—say, if we wuz setin' in jedgment then?

Why, we'd jest kind uv bresh the moisture from our eyes 'nd say: "Mister recordin' angel, you may nolly pros this case 'nd perseed with the docket."

CHAPTER XVIII

THE LITTLE YALLER BABY

I hev allus hed a good opinion uv the wimmin folks. I don't look at 'em as some people do; uv course they're a necessity—just as men are. Uv course if there warn't no wimmin folks there wouldn't be no men folks—leastwise that's what the medikil books say. But I never wuz much on discussin' humin economy; what I hev allus thought 'nd said wuz that wimmin folks wuz a kind uv luxury, 'nd the best kind, too. Maybe it's because I haint hed much to do with 'em that I'm sot on 'em. Never did get real well acquainted with more 'n three or four uv 'em in all my life; seemed like it wuz meant that I shouldn't hev 'em round me as most men hev. Mother died when I wuz a little tyke, an' Ant Mary raised me till I wuz big enuff to make my own livin'. Down here in the Southwest, you see, most uv the girls is boys; there aint none uv them civilizin' influences folks talk uv,—nothin' but flowers 'nd birds 'nd such things as poetry tells about. So I kind uv growed up with the curis notion that wimmin folks wuz too good for our part uv the country, 'nd I hevn't quite got that notion out'n my head yet.

One time—wall, I reckon 't wuz about four years ago—I got a letter frum ol' Col. Sibley to come up to Saint Louey 'nd consult with him 'bout some stock int'rests we hed together. Railroad travellin' wuz no new thing to me. I hed been prutty posperous,—hed got past hevin' to ride in a caboose 'nd git out at every stop to punch up the steers. Hed money in the Hoost'n bank 'nd use to go to Tchicargo oncet a year; hed met Fill Armer 'nd shook hands with him, 'nd oncet the city papers hed a colume article about my bein' a millionnaire; uv course 't warn't so, but a feller kind uv likes that sort uv thing, you know.

The mornin' after I got that letter from Col. Sibley I started for Saint Louey. I took a bunk in the Pullman car, like I hed been doin' for six years past; 'nd I reckon the other folks must hev thought I wuz a heap uv a man, for every haff-hour I give the nigger haf a dollar to bresh me off. The car wuz full uv people,—rich people, too, I reckon, for they wore good clo'es 'nd criticised the scenery. Jest across frum me there wuz a lady with a big, fat baby,—the pruttiest woman I hed seen in a month uv Sundays; and the baby! why, doggone my skin, when I wuzn't payin' money to the nigger, darned if I didn't set there watchin' the big, fat little cuss, like he wuz the only baby I ever seen. I aint much of a hand at babies, 'cause I haint seen many uv 'em, 'nd when it comes to handlin' 'em—why, that would break me all up, 'nd like 's not 't would break the baby all up too. But it has allus been my notion that nex' to the wimmin folks babies wuz jest about the nicest things on earth. So the more I looked at that big, fat little baby settin' in its mother's lap 'cross the way, the more I wanted to look; seemed like I wuz hoodooed by the little tyke; 'nd the first thing I knew there wuz water in my eyes; don't know why it is, but it allus makes me kind ur slop over to set 'nd watch a baby cooin' 'nd playin' in its mother's lap.

"Look a' hyar, Sam," says I to the nigger, "come hyar 'nd bresh me off agin! Why aint you tendin' to bizniss?"

But it didn't do no good 't all; pertendin' to be cross with the nigger might fool the other folks in the car, but it didn't fool me. I wuz dead stuck on that baby—gol durn his pictur'! And there the little tyke set in its mother's lap, doublin' up its fists 'nd tryin' to swaller 'em, 'nd talkin' like to its mother in a lingo I couldn't understan', but which the mother could, for she talked back to the baby in a soothin' lingo which I couldn't understand but which I liked to hear, 'nd she kissed the baby 'nd stroked its hair 'nd petted it like wimmin do.

It made me mad to hear them other folks in the car criticisn' the scenery 'nd things. A man's in mighty poor bizness, anyhow, to be lookin' at scenery when there's a woman in sight,—a woman and a baby!

Prutty soon—oh, maybe in a hour or two—the baby began to fret 'nd worrit. Seemed to me like the little critter wuz hungry. Knowin' that there wuzn't no eatin'-house this side uv Bowieville, I jest called the train boy, 'nd says I to him: "Hev you got any victuals that will do for a baby?"

"How is oranges 'nd bananas?" says he.

"That ought to do," sez I. "Jist do up a dozen uv your best oranges 'nd a dozen uv your best bananas 'nd take 'em over to that baby with my complerments."

But before he could do it, the lady hed laid the baby on one uv her arms 'nd hed spread a shawl over its head 'nd over her shoulder, 'nd all uv a suddin' the baby quit worritin' and seemed like he hed gone to sleep.

When we got to York Crossin' I looked out'n the winder 'nd seen some men carryin' a long pine box up towards the baggage car. Seein' their hats off, I knew there wuz a dead body in the box, 'nd I couldn't help feelin' sorry for the poor creetur that hed died in that lonely place uv York Crossin'; but I mought hev felt a heap sorrier for the creeters that hed to live there, for I'll allow that York Crossin' is a leetle the durnedest lonesomest place I ever seen.

Well, just afore the train started agin, who should come into the car but Bill Woodson, and he wuz lookin' powerful tough. Bill herded cattle for me three winters, but hed moved away when he married one uv the waiter girls at Spooner's hotel at Hoost'n.

"Hello, Bill," says I; "what air you totin' so kind uv keerful-like in your arms there?"

"Why, I've got the baby," says he; 'nd as he said it the tears come up into his eyes.

"Your own baby, Bill?" says I.

"Yes," says he. "Nellie took sick uv the janders a fortnight ago, 'nd—'nd she died, 'nd I'm takin' her body up to Texarkany to bury. She lived there, you know, 'nd I'm goin' to leave the baby there with its gran'ma."

Poor Bill! it wuz his wife that the men were carryin' in that pine box to the baggage car.

"Likely lookin' baby, Bill," says I, cheerful like. "Perfect pictur' uv its mother; kind uv favors you round the lower part uv the face, tho'."

I said this to make Bill feel happier. If I'd told the truth, I'd 've said the baby wuz a sickly, yaller-lookin' little thing, for so it wuz; looked haff-starved, too. Couldn't help comparin' it with that big, fat baby in its mother's arms over the way.

"Bill," says I, "here's a ten-dollar note for the baby, 'nd God bless you!"

"Thank ye, Mr. Goodhue," says he, 'nd he choked all up as he moved off with that yaller little baby in his arms. It warn't very fur up the road he wuz goin', 'nd he found a seat in one uv the front cars.

But along about an hour after that back come Bill, moseyin' through the car like he wuz huntin' for somebody. Seemed like he wuz in trubble and wuz huntin' for a friend.

"Anything I kin do for you, Bill?" says I, but he didn't make no answer. All of a suddint he sot his eyes on the prutty lady that had the fat baby sleepin' in her arms, 'nd he made a break for her like he wuz crazy. He took off his hat 'nd bent down over her 'nd said somethin' none uv the rest uv us could hear. The lady kind uv started like she wuz frightened, 'nd then she looked up at Bill 'nd looked him right square in the countenance. She saw a tall, ganglin', awkward man, with long yaller hair 'nd frowzy beard, 'nd she saw that he wuz tremblin' 'nd hed tears in his eyes. She looked down at the fat baby in her arms, 'nd then she looked out'n the winder at the great stretch uv prairie land, 'nd seemed like she wuz lookin' off further'n the rest uv us could see. Then, at last, she turnt around 'nd said, "Yes," to Bill, 'nd Bill went off into the front car ag'in.

None uv the rest uv us knew what all this meant, but in a minnit Bill come back with his little yaller baby in his arms, 'nd you never heerd a baby squall 'nd carry on like that baby wuz squallin' 'nd carryin' on. Fact is, the little yaller baby was hungry, hungrier'n a wolf, 'nd there wuz its mother dead in the car up ahead 'nd its gran'ma a good piece up the road. What did the lady over the way do but lay her own sleepin' baby down on the seat beside her 'nd take Bill's little yaller baby 'nd hold it on one arm 'nd cover up its head 'nd her shoulder with a shawl, jist like she had done with the fat baby not long afore. Bill never looked at her; he took off his hat and held it in his hand, 'nd turnt around 'nd stood guard over that mother, 'nd I reckon that ef any man hed darst to look that way jist then Bill would've cut his heart out.

The little yaller baby didn't cry very long. Seemed like it knowed there wuz a mother holdin' it,—not its own mother, but a woman whose life hed been hallowed by God's blessin' with the love 'nd the purity 'nd the sanctity uv motherhood.

Why, I wouldn't hev swapped that sight uv Bill an' them two babies 'nd that sweet woman for all the cattle in Texas! It jest made me know that what I'd allus thought uv wimmin was gospel truth. God bless that lady! I say, wherever she is to-day, 'nd God bless all wimmin folks, for they're all alike in their unselfishness 'nd gentleness 'nd love!

Bill said, "God bless ye!" too, when she handed him back his poor little yaller baby. The little creeter wuz fast asleep, 'nd Bill darsent speak very loud for fear he'd wake it up. But his heart wuz way up in his mouth when he says "God bless ye!" to that dear lady; 'nd then he added, like he wanted to let her know that he meant to pay her back when he could: "I'll do the same for you some time, marm, if I kin."

CHAPTER XIX

THE CYCLOPEEDY

Havin' lived next door to the Hobart place f'r goin' on thirty years, I calc'late that I know jest about ez much about the case ez anybody else now on airth, exceptin' perhaps it's ol' Jedge Baker, and he's so plaguey old 'nd so powerful feeble that he don't know nothin'.

It seems that in the spring uv '47—the year that Cy Watson's oldest boy wuz drownded in West River—there come along a book agent sellin' volyumes 'nd tracks f'r the diffusion uv knowledge, 'nd havin' got the recommend of the minister 'nd uv the select men, he done an all-fired big business in our part uv the county. His name wuz Lemuel Higgins, 'nd he wuz ez likely a talker ez I ever heerd, barrin' Lawyer Conkey, 'nd everybody allowed that when Conkey wuz round he talked so fast that the town pump ud have to be greased every twenty minutes.

One of the first uv our folks that this Lemuel Higgins struck wuz Leander Hobart. Leander had jest marr'd one uv the Peasley girls, 'nd had moved into the old homestead on the Plainville road,—old Deacon Hobart havin' give up the place to him, the other boys havin' moved out West (like a lot o' darned fools that they wuz!). Leander wuz feelin' his oats jest about this time, 'nd nuthin' wuz too good f'r him.

"Hattie," sez he, "I guess I'll have to lay in a few books f'r readin' in the winter time, 'nd I've half a notion to subscribe f'r a cyclopeedy. Mr. Higgins here says they're invalerable in a family, and that we orter have 'em, bein' as how we're likely to have the fam'ly bime by."

"Lor's sakes, Leander, how you talk!" sez Hattie, blushin' all over, ez brides allers does to heern tell uv sich things.

Waal, to make a long story short, Leander bargained with Mr. Higgins for a set uv them cyclopeedies, 'nd he signed his name to a long printed paper that showed how he agreed to take a cyclopeedy oncet in so often, which wuz to be ez often ez a new one uv the volyumes wuz printed. A cyclopeedy isn't printed all at oncet, because that would make it cost too much; consekently the man that gets it up has it strung along fur apart, so as to hit folks oncet every year or two, and gin'rally about harvest time. So Leander kind uv liked the idee, and he signed the printed paper 'nd made his affidavit to it afore Jedge Warner.

The fust volyume of the cyclopeedy stood on a shelf in the old seckertary in the settin'-room about four months before they had any use f'r it. One night 'Squire Turner's son come over to visit Leander 'nd Hattie, and they got to talkin' about apples, 'nd the sort uv apples that wuz the best. Leander allowed that the Rhode Island greenin' wuz the best, but Hattie and the Turner boy stuck up f'r the Roxbury russet, until at last a happy idee struck Leander, and sez he: "We'll leave it to the cyclopeedy, b'gosh! Whichever one the cyclopeedy sez is the best will settle it."

"But you can't find out nothin' 'bout Roxbury russets nor Rhode Island greenin's in our cyclopeedy," sez Hattie.

"Why not, I'd like to know?" sez Leander, kind uv indignant like.

"'Cause ours haint got down to the R yet," sez Hattie. "All ours tells about is things beginnin' with A."

"Well, aint we talkin' about Apples?" sez Leander. "You aggervate me terrible, Hattie, by insistin' on knowin' what you don't know nothin' 'bout."

Leander went to the seckertary 'nd took down the cyclopeedy 'nd hunted all through it f'r Apples, but all he could find wuz "Apple—See Pomology."

"How in thunder kin I see Pomology," sez Leander, "when there aint no Pomology to see? Gol durn a cyclopeedy, anyhow!"

And he put the volyume back onto the shelf 'nd never sot eyes into it agin.

That's the way the thing run f'r years 'nd years. Leander would've gin up the plaguey bargain, but he couldn't; he had signed a printed paper 'nd had swore to it afore a justice of the peace. Higgins would have had the law on him if he had throwed up the trade.

The most aggervatin' feature uv it all wuz that a new one uv them cussid cyclopeedies wuz allus sure to show up at the wrong time,—when Leander wuz hard up or had jest been afflicted some way or other. His barn burnt down two nights afore the volyume containin' the letter B arrived, and Leander needed all his chink to pay f'r lumber, but Higgins sot back on that affidavit and defied the life out uv him.

"Never mind, Leander," sez his wife, soothin' like, "it's a good book to have in the house, anyhow, now that we've got a baby."

"That's so," sez Leander, "babies does begin with B, don't it?"

You see their fust baby had been born; they named him Peasley,—Peasley Hobart,—after Hattie's folks. So, seein' as how it wuz payin' f'r a book that told about babies, Leander didn't begredge that five dollars so very much after all.

"Leander," sez Hattie one forenoon, "that B cyclopeedy aint no account. There aint nothin' in it about babies except 'See Maternity'!"

"Waal, I'll be gosh durned!" sez Leander. That wuz all he said, and he couldn't do nothin' at all, f'r that book agent, Lemuel Higgins, had the dead wood on him,—the mean, sneakin' critter!

So the years passed on, one of them cyclopeedies showin' up now 'nd then,—sometimes every two years 'nd sometimes every four, but allus at a time when Leander found it pesky hard to give up a fiver. It warn't no use cussin' Higgins; Higgins just laffed when Leander allowed that the cyclopeedy wuz no good 'nd that he wuz bein' robbed. Meantime Leander's family wuz increasin' and growin'. Little Sarey had the hoopin' cough dreadful one winter, but the cyclopeedy didn't help out at all, 'cause all it said wuz: "Hoopin' Cough—See Whoopin' Cough"—and uv course, there warn't no Whoopin' Cough to see, bein' as how the W hadn't come yet!

Oncet when Hiram wanted to dreen the home pasture, he went to the cyclopeedy to find out about it, but all he diskivered wuz: "Drain—See Tile." This wuz in 1859, and the cyclopeedy had only got down to G.

The cow wuz sick with lung fever one spell, and Leander laid her dyin' to that cussid cyclopeedy, 'cause when he went to readin' 'bout cows it told him to "See Zoölogy."

But what's the use uv harrowin' up one's feelin's talkin' 'nd thinkin' about these things? Leander got so after a while that the cyclopeedy didn't worry him at all: he grew to look at it ez one uv the crosses that human critters has to bear without complainin' through this vale uv tears. The only thing that bothered him wuz the fear that mebbe he wouldn't live to see the last volume,—to tell the truth, this kind uv got to be his hobby, and I've heern him talk 'bout it many a time settin' round the stove at the tarvern 'nd squirtin' tobacco juice at the sawdust box. His wife, Hattie, passed away with the yaller janders the winter W come, and all that seemed to reconcile Leander to survivin' her wuz the prospect uv seein' the last volyume uv that cyclopeedy. Lemuel Higgins, the book agent, had gone to his everlastin' punishment; but his son, Hiram, had succeeded to his father's business 'nd continued to visit the folks his old man had roped in. By this time Leander's children had growed up; all on 'em wuz marr'd, and there wuz numeris grandchildren to amuse the ol' gentleman. But Leander wuzn't to be satisfied with the common things uv airth; he didn't seem to take no pleasure in his grandchildren like most men do; his mind wuz allers sot on somethin' else,—for hours 'nd hours, yes, all day long, he'd set out on the front stoop lookin' wistfully up the road for that book agent to come along with a cyclopeedy. He didn't want to die till he'd got all the cyclopeedies his contract called for; he wanted to have everything straightened out before he passed away.

When—oh, how well I recollect it—when Y come along he wuz so overcome that he fell over in a fit uv paralysis, 'nd the old gentleman never got over it. For the next three years he drooped 'nd pined, and seemed like he couldn't hold out much longer. Finally he had to take to his bed,—he was so old 'nd feeble,—but he made 'em move the bed up aginst the winder so he could watch for that last volyume of the cyclopeedy.

The end come one balmy day in the spring uv '87. His life wuz a-ebbin' powerful fast; the minister wuz there, 'nd me, 'nd Dock Wilson, 'nd Jedge Baker, 'nd most uv the fam'ly. Lovin' hands smoothed the wrinkled forehead 'nd breshed back the long, scant, white hair, but the eyes of the dyin' man wuz sot upon that piece uv road down which the cyclopeedy man allus come.

All to oncet a bright 'nd joyful look come into them eyes, 'nd ol' Leander riz up in bed 'nd sez, "It's come!"

"What is it, Father?" asked his daughter Sarey, sobbin' like.

"Hush," sez the minister, solemnly; "he sees the shinin' gates uv the Noo Jerusalum."

"No, no," cried the aged man; "it is the cyclopeedy—the letter Z—it's comin'!"

And, sure enough! the door opened, and in walked Higgins. He tottered rather than walked, f'r he had growed old 'nd feeble in his wicked perfession.

"Here's the Z cyclopeedy, Mr. Hobart," says Higgins.

Leander clutched it; he hugged it to his pantin' bosom; then stealin' one pale hand under the piller he drew out a faded bank-note 'nd gave it to Higgins.

"I thank Thee for this boon," sez Leander, rollin' his eyes up devoutly; then he gave a deep sigh.

"Hold on," cried Higgins, excitedly, "you've made a mistake—it isn't the last—"

But Leander didn't hear him—his soul hed fled from its mortal tenement 'nd hed soared rejoicin' to realms uv everlastin' bliss.

"He is no more," sez Dock Wilson, metaphorically.

"Then who are his heirs?" asked that mean critter Higgins.

"We be," sez the family.

"Do you conjointly and severally acknowledge and assume the obligation of deceased to me?" he asked 'em.

"What obligation?" asked Peasley Hobart, stern like.

"Deceased died owin' me f'r a cyclopeedy!" sez Higgins.

"That's a lie!" sez Peasley. "We all seen him pay you for the Z!"

"But there's another one to come," sez Higgins.

"Another?" they all asked.

"Yes, the index!" sez he.

So there wuz, and I'll be eternally goll durned if he aint a-suin' the estate in the probate court now f'r the price uv it!

CHAPTER XX

DOCK STEBBINS

Most everybody liked Dock Stebbins, fur all he wuz the durnedest critter that ever lived to play jokes on folks! Seems like he wuz born jokin' 'nd kep' it up all his life. Ol' Mrs. Stebbins used to tell how when the Dock wuz a baby he use to wake her up haff a dozen times un a night cryin' like he wuz hungry, 'nd when she turnt over in bed to him he wud laff 'nd coo like he wuz sayin', "No, thank ye— I wuz only foolin'!"

His mother allus thought a heap uv the Dock, 'nd she allus put up with his jokes 'nd things without grumblin'; said it warn't his fault that he wuz so full uv tricks 'nd funny business; kind uv took the responsibility uv it onto herself, because, as she allowed, she'd been to a circus jest afore he wuz born.

Nothin' tickled the Dock more 'n to worry folks,—not in a mean way, but jest to sort uv bother 'em. Use to hang round the post-office 'nd pertend to have fits,—sakes alive! but how that scared the women folks. One day who should come along but ol' Sue Perkins; Sue wuz suspicioned of takin' a nip uv likker on the quiet now 'nd then, but nobody had ever ketched her at it. Wall, the Dock he had one uv his fits jest as Sue hove in sight, 'nd Lem Thompson (who stood in with Dock in all his deviltry) leant over Dock while he wuz wallerin' 'nd pertending to foam at the mouth, and Lem cried out: "Nothink will fetch him out'n this turn but a drink uv brandy." Sue, who wuz as kind-hearted a old maid as ever superntended a strawberry festival, whipped a bottle out'n her bag 'nd says: "Here you be, Lem, but don't let him swaller the bottle." Folks bothered Sue a heap 'bout this joke till she moved down into Texas to teach school.

Dock had a piece uv wood 'bout two inches long,—maybe three: it wuz black 'nd stubby 'nd looked jest like the butt uv a cigar. Nobody but Dock wud ever hev thought uv sech a fool thing, but Dock use to go round with that thing in his mouth like it wuz a cigar, and when he'd meet a man who wuz smokin' he'd say: "Excuse me, but will you please to gimme a light?" Then the man wud hand over his cigar, and Dock wud plough that wood stub uv his'n around in the lighted cigar and would pretend to puff away till he had put the real cigar out, 'nd then Dock wud hand the cigar back, sayin', kind uv regretful like: "You don't seem to have much uv a light there; I reckon I'll wait till I kin git a match." You kin imagine how that other feller's cigar tasted when he lighted it agin. Dock tried it on me oncet, 'nd when I lighted up agin seemed like I wuz smokin' a piece uv rope or a liver pad.

One time Dock 'nd Lem Thompson went over to Peory on the railroad, 'nd while they wuz settin' in the car in come two wimmin 'nd set in the seat ahead uv 'em. All uv a suddint Dock nudged Lem and sez, jest loud enuff fur the wimmin to hear: "I didn't git round till after it wuz over, but I never see sech a sight as that baby's ear wuz."

Lem wuz onto Dock's methods, 'nd he knew there wuz sumthin' ahead. So he says: "Tough-lookin' ear, wuz it?"

"Wall, I should remark," says Dock. "You see it wuz like this: the mother had gone out into the back yard to hang some clo'es onto the line, 'nd she laid the baby down in the crib. Baby wan't more 'n six weeks old,—helpless little critter as ever you seen. Wall, all to oncet the mother heerd the baby cryin', but bein' busy with them clo'es she didn't mind much. The baby kep' cryin' 'nd cryin', 'nd at last the mother come back into the house, 'nd there she found a big rat gnawin' at one uv the baby's ears,—had et it nearly off! There lay that helpless little innocent, cryin' 'nd writhin', 'nd there sat that rat with his long tail, nippin' 'nd chewin' at one uv them tiny coral ears—oh, it wuz offul!"

"Jest imagine the feelinks uv the mother!" says Lem, sad like.

"Jest imagine the feelinks uv the baby," sez Dock. "How'd you like to be lyin' helpless in a crib with a big rat gnawin' your ear?"

Wall, all this conversation wuz fur from pleasant to those two wimmin in the front seat, fur wimmin love babies 'nd hate rats, you know. It wuz nuts fur Dock 'nd Lem to see the two wimmin squirm, 'nd all the way to Peory they didn't talk about nuthink but snakes 'nd spiders 'nd mice 'nd caterpillers. When the train got to Peory a gentleman met the two wimmin 'nd sez to one uv 'em: "I'm feered the trip haint done you much good, Lizzie," says he. "Sakes alive, John," says she, "it's a wonder we haint dead, for we've been travellin' forty miles with a real live Beadle dime novvell!"

'Nuther trick Dock had wuz to walk 'long the street behind wimmin 'nd tell about how his sister had jest lost one uv her diamond earrings while out walkin'. Jest as soon as the wimmin heerd this they'd clap their han's up to their ears to see if their earrings wuz all right. Dock never laffed nor let on like he wuz jokin', but jest the same this sort uv thing tickled him nearly to deth.

Dock went up to Chicago with Jedge Craig oncet, 'nd when they come back the jedge said he'd never had such an offul time in all his born days. Said that Dock bought a fool Mother Goose book to read in the hoss-cars jest to queer folks; would set in a hoss-car lookin' at the picturs 'nd readin' the verses 'nd laffin' like it wuz all new to him 'nd like he wuz a child. Everybody sized him up for a ejeot, 'nd the wimmin folks shook their heads 'nd said it wuz orful fur so fine a lookin' feller to be such a tom fool. 'Nuther thing Dock did wuz to git hold uv a bad quarter 'nd give it to a beggar, 'nd then foller the beggar into a saloon 'nd git him arrested for tryin' to pass counterfit money. I reckon that if Dock had stayed in Chicago a week he'd have had everybody crazy.

No, I don't know how he come to be a medikil man. He told me oncet that when he found out that he wuzn't good for anythink he concluded he'd be a doctor; but I reckon that wuz one uv his jokes. He didn't have much uv a practice: he wuz too yumorous to suit most invalids 'nd sick folks. We had him tend our boy Sam jest oncet when Sam wuz comin' down with the measles. He looked at Sam's tongue 'nd felt his pulse 'nd said he'd leave a pill for Sam to take afore goin' to bed.

"How shell we administer the pill?" asked my wife.

"Wall," says Dock, "the best way to do is to git the boy down on the floor 'nd hold his mouth open 'nd gag him till he swallers the pill. After the pill gits into his system it will explode in about ten minits, 'nd then the boy will feel better."

This wuz cheerful news for the boy. No human power cud ha' got that pill into Sam. We never solicited Dock's perfeshional services agin.

One time Dock 'nd Lem Thompson drove over to Knoxville to help Dock Parsons cut a man's leg off. About four miles out uv town 'nd right in the middle uv the hot peraroor they met Moses Baker's oldest boy trudgin' along with a basket uf eggs. The Dock whoaed his hoss 'nd called to the boy,—

"Where be you goin' with them eggs?" says he.

"Goin' to town to sell 'em," says the boy.

"How much a dozen?" asked the Dock.

"'Bout ten cents, I reckon," says the boy.

"Putty likely-lookin' eggs," says the Dock; 'nd he handed the lines over to Lem, 'nd got out'n the buggy.

"How many hev you got?" he asked.

"Ten dozen," says the boy.

"Git out!" says Dock. "There haint no ten dozen eggs in that basket!"

"Yes, there is," says the boy, "fur I counted 'em myself."

The Dock allowed that he wuzn't goin' to take nobody's count on eggs; so he got that fool boy to stan' there in the middle uv that hot peraroor, claspin' his two hands together, while he, the Dock, counted them eggs out'n the basket one by one into the boy's arms. Ten dozen eggs is a heap; you kin imagine, maybe, how that boy looked with his arms full uv eggs! When the Dock had got about nine dozen counted out he stopped all uv a suddint 'nd said, "Wall, come to think on 't, I reckon I don't want no eggs to-day, but I'm jest as much obleeged to you fur yer trouble." And so he jumped back into the buggy 'nd drove off.

Now, maybe that fool boy wuzn't in a peck uv trubble! There he stood in the middle uv that hot— that all-fired hot—peraroor with his arms full uv eggs. What wuz there fur him to do? He wuz afraid to move, lest he should break them eggs; yet the longer he stood there the less chance there wuz of the warm weather improvin' the eggs.

Along in the summer of '78 the fever broke out down South, 'nd one day Dock made up his mind that as bizness wuzn't none too good at home he'd go down South 'nd see what he could do there. That wuz jest like one of Dock's fool notions, we all said. But he went. In about six weeks along come a telegraph sayin' that Dock wuz dead,—he'd died uv the fever. The minister went up to the homestead 'nd broke the news gentle like to Dock's mother; but, bless you! she didn't believe it— she wouldn't believe it. She said it wuz one uv Dock's jokes; she didn't blame him, nuther—it wuz her fault, she allowed, that Dock wuz allus that way about makin' fun uv life 'nd death. No, sir; she never believed that Dock wuz dead, but she allus talked like he might come in any minnit; and there wuz allus his old place set fur him at the table 'nd nuthin' was disturbed in his little room upstairs. And so five years slipped by 'nd no Dock come back, 'nd there wuz no tidin's uv him. Uv course, the rest uv us knew; but his mother—oh, no, she never would believe it.

At last the old lady fell sick, and the doctor said she couldn't hold out long, she wuz so old 'nd feeble. The minister who wuz there said that she seemed to sleep from the evenin' of this life into the mornin' uv the next. Jest afore the last she kind uv raised up in bed and cried out like she saw sumthin' that she loved, and she held out her arms like there wuz some one standin' in the doorway. Then they asked her what the matter wuz, and she says, joyful like: "He's come back, and there he stan's jest as he use ter: I knew he wuz only jokin'!"

They looked, but they saw nuthin'; 'nd when they went to her she wuz dead.

CHAPTER XXI

THE FAIRIES OF PESTH

An old poet walked alone in a quiet valley. His heart was heavy, and the voices of Nature consoled him. His life had been a lonely and sad one. Many years ago a great grief fell upon him, and it took away all his joy and all his ambition. It was because he brooded over his sorrow, and because he was always faithful to a memory, that the townspeople deemed him a strange old poet; but they loved him and they loved his songs,—in his life and in his songs there was a gentleness, a sweetness, a pathos that touched every heart. "The strange, the dear old poet," they called him.

Evening was coming on. The birds made no noise; only the whip-poor-will repeated over and over again its melancholy refrain in the marsh beyond the meadow. The brook ran slowly, and its voice was so hushed and tiny that you might have thought that it was saying its prayers before going to bed.

The old poet came to the three lindens. This was a spot he loved, it was so far from the noise of the town. The grass under the lindens was fresh and velvety. The air was full of fragrance, for here amid the grass grew violets and daisies and buttercups and other modest wildflowers. Under the lindens stood old Leeza, the witchwife.

"Take this," said the poet to old Leeza, the witchwife; and he gave her a silver-piece.

"You are good to me, master poet," said the witchwife. "You have always been good to me. I do not forget, master poet, I do not forget."

"Why do you speak so strangely?" asked the old poet. "You mean more than you say. Do not jest with me; my heart is heavy with sorrow."

"I do not jest," answered the witchwife. "I will show you a strange thing. Do as I bid you; tarry here under the lindens, and when the moon rises, the Seven Crickets will chirp thrice; then the Raven will fly into the west, and you will see wonderful things, and beautiful things you will hear."

Saying this much, old Leeza, the witchwife, stole away, and the poet marvelled at her words. He had heard the townspeople say that old Leeza was full of dark thoughts and of evil deeds, but he did not heed these stories.

"They say the same of me, perhaps," he thought. "I will tarry here beneath the three lindens and see what may come of this whereof the witchwife spake."

The old poet sat amid the grass at the foot of the three lindens, and darkness fell around him. He could see the lights in the town away off; they twinkled like the stars that studded the sky. The whip-poor-will told his story over and over again in the marsh beyond the meadow, and the brook tossed and talked in its sleep, for it had played too hard that day.

"The moon is rising," said the old poet. "Now we shall see."

The moon peeped over the tops of the far-off hills. She wondered whether the world was fast asleep. She peeped again. There could be no doubt; the world was fast asleep,—at least so thought the dear old moon. So she stepped boldly up from behind the distant hills. The stars were glad that she came, for she was indeed a merry old moon.

The Seven Crickets lived in the hedge. They were brothers, and they made famous music. When they saw the moon in the sky they sang "chirp-chirp, chirp-chirp, chirp-chirp," three times, just as old Leeza, the witchwife, said they would.

"Whir-r-r!" It was the Raven flying out of the oak-tree into the west. This, too, was what the old witchwife had foretold. "Whir-r-r" went the two black wings, and then it seemed as if the Raven melted into the night. Now, this was strange enough, but what followed was stranger still.

Hardly had the Raven flown away, when out from their habitations in the moss, the flowers, and the grass trooped a legion of fairies,—yes, right there before the old poet's eyes appeared, as if by magic, a mighty troop of the dearest little fays in all the world.

Each of these fairies was about the height of a cambric needle. The lady fairies were, of course, not so tall as the gentleman fairies, but all were of quite as comely figure as you could expect to find even among real folk. They were quaintly dressed; the ladies wearing quilted silk gowns and broad-brim hats with tiny feathers in them, and the gentlemen wearing curious little knickerbockers, with silk coats, white hose, ruffled shirts, and dainty cocked hats.

"If the witchwife had not foretold it I should say that I dreamed," thought the old poet. But he was not frightened. He had never harmed the fairies, therefore he feared no evil from them.

One of the fairies was taller than the rest, and she was much more richly attired. It was not her crown alone that showed her to be the queen. The others made obeisance to her as she passed through the midst of them from her home in the bunch of red clover. Four dainty pages preceded her, carrying a silver web which had been spun by a black-and-yellow garden spider of great renown. This silver web the four pages spread carefully over a violet leaf, and thereupon the queen sat down. And when she was seated the queen sang this little song:

"From the land of murk and mist
Fairy folk are coming
To the mead the dew has kissed,
And they dance where'er they list
To the cricket's thrumming.

"Circling here and circling there,
Light as thought and free as air,
Hear them cry, 'Oho, oho,'
As they round the rosey go.

"Appleblossom, Summerdew,
Thistleblow, and Ganderfeather!
Join the airy fairy crew
Dancing on the sward together!
Till the cock on yonder steeple
Gives all faery lusty warning,
Sing and dance, my little people,—
Dance and sing 'Oho' till morning!"

The four little fairies the queen called to must have been loitering. But now they came scampering up,—Ganderfeather behind the others, for he was a very fat and presumably a very lazy little fairy.

"The elves will be here presently," said the queen, "and then, little folk, you shall dance to your heart's content. Dance your prettiest to-night for the good old poet is watching you."

"Ah, little queen," cried the old poet, "you see me, then? I thought to watch your revels unbeknown to you. But I meant you no disrespect,—indeed, I meant you none, for surely no one ever loved the little folk more than I."

"We know you love us, good old poet," said the little fairy queen, "and this night shall give you great joy and bring you into wondrous fame."

These were words of which the old poet knew not the meaning; but we, who live these many years after he has fallen asleep,—we know the meaning of them.

Then, surely enough, the elves came trooping along. They lived in the further meadow, else they had come sooner. They were somewhat larger than the fairies, yet they were very tiny and very delicate creatures. The elf prince had long flaxen curls, and he was arrayed in a wonderful suit of damask web, at the manufacture of which seventy-seven silkworms had labored for seventy-seven days, receiving in payment therefor as many mulberry leaves as seven blue beetles could carry and stow in seven times seven sunny days. At his side the elf prince wore a sword made of the sting of a yellow-jacket, and the hilt of this sword was studded with the eyes of unhatched dragon-flies, these brighter and more precious than the most costly diamonds.

The elf prince sat beside the fairy queen. The other elves capered around among the fairies. The dancing sward was very light, for a thousand and ten glowworms came from the marsh and hung their beautiful lamps over the spot where the little folk were assembled. If the moon and the stars were jealous of that soft, mellow light, they had good reason to be.

The fairies and elves circled around in lively fashion. Their favorite dance was the ring-round-a-rosy which many children nowadays dance. But they had other measures, too, and they danced them very prettily.

"I wish," said the old poet, "I wish that I had my violin here, for then I would make merry music for you."

The fairy queen laughed. "We have music of our own," she said, "and it is much more beautiful than even you, dear old poet, could make."

Then, at the queen's command, each gentleman elf offered his arm to a lady fairy, and each gentleman fairy offered his arm to a lady elf, and so, all being provided with partners, these little people took their places for a waltz. The fairy queen and the elf prince were the only ones that did not dance; they sat side by side on the violet leaf and watched the others. The hoptoad was floor manager; the green burdock badge on his breast showed that.

"Mind where you go—don't jostle each other," cried the hoptoad, for he was an exceedingly methodical fellow, despite his habit of jumping at conclusions.

Then, when all was ready, the Seven Crickets went "chirp-chirp, chirp-chirp, chirp-chirp," three times, and away flew that host of little fairies and little elves in the daintiest waltz imaginable:—

The old poet was delighted. Never before had he seen such a sight; never before had he heard so sweet music. Round and round whirled the sprite dancers; the thousand and ten glowworms caught the rhythm of the music that floated up to them, and they swung their lamps to and fro in time with the fairy waltz. The plumes in the hats of the cunning little ladies nodded hither and thither, and the tiny swords of the cunning little gentlemen bobbed this way and that as the throng of dancers swept now here, now there. With one tiny foot, upon which she wore a lovely shoe made of a tanned flea's hide, the fairy queen beat time, yet she heard every word which the gallant elf prince said. So, with the fairy queen blushing, the mellow lamps swaying, the elf prince wooing, and the throng of little folk dancing hither and thither, the fairy music went on and on:—

"Tell me, my fairy queen," cried the old poet, "whence comes this fairy music which I hear? The Seven Crickets in the hedge are still, the birds sleep in their nests, the brook dreams of the mountain home it stole away from yester morning. Tell me, therefore, whence comes this wondrous fairy music, and show me the strange musicians that make it."

"Look to the grass and the flowers," said the fairy queen. "In every blade and in every bud lie hidden notes of fairy music. Each violet and daisy and buttercup,—every modest wild-flower (no matter how hidden) gives glad response to the tinkle of fairy feet. Dancing daintily over this quiet sward where flowers dot the green, my little people strike here and there and everywhere the keys which give forth the harmonies you hear."

Long marvelled the old poet. He forgot his sorrow, for the fairy music stole into his heart and soothed the wound there. The fairy host swept round and round, and the fairy music went on and on.

"Why may I not dance?" asked a piping voice. "Please, dear queen, may I not dance, too?"

It was the little hunchback that spake,—the little hunchback fairy who, with wistful eyes, had been watching the merry throng whirl round and round.

"Dear child, thou canst not dance," said the fairy queen, tenderly; "thy little limbs are weak. Come, sit thou at my feet, and let me smooth thy fair curls and stroke thy pale cheeks."

"Believe me, dear queen," persisted the little hunchback, "I can dance, and quite prettily, too. Many a time while the others made merry here I have stolen away by myself to the brookside and danced alone in the moonlight,—alone with my shadow. The violets are thickest there. 'Let thy halting feet fall upon us, Little Sorrowful,' they whispered, 'and we shall make music for thee.' So there I danced, and the violets sang their songs for me. I could hear the others making merry far away, but I was merry, too; for I, too, danced, and there was none to laugh."

"If you would like it, Little Sorrowful," said the elf prince, "I will dance with you."

"No, brave prince," answered the little hunchback, "for that would weary you. My crutch is stout, and it has danced with me before. You will say that we dance very prettily,—my crutch and I,—and you will not laugh, I know."

Then the queen smiled sadly; she loved the little hunchback and she pitied her.

"It shall be as you wish," said the queen. The little hunchback was overjoyed.

"I have to catch the time, you see," said she, and she tapped her crutch and swung one little shrunken foot till her body fell into the rhythm of the waltz.

Far daintier than the others did the little hunchback dance; now one tiny foot and now the other tinkled on the flowers, and the point of the little crutch fell here and there like a tear. And as she danced, there crept into the fairy music a tenderer cadence, for (I know not why) the little hunchback danced ever on the violets, and their responses were full of the music of tears. There was a strange pathos in the little creature's grace; she did not weary of the dance: her cheeks flushed, and her eyes grew fuller, and there was a wondrous light in them. And as the little hunchback danced, the others forgot her limp and felt only the heart-cry in the little hunchback's merriment and in the music of the voiceful violets.

Now all this saw the old poet, and all this wondrously beautiful music he heard. And as he heard and saw these things, he thought of the pale face, the weary eyes, and the tired little body that slept forever now. He thought of the voice that had tried to be cheerful for his sake, of the thin, patient little hands that had loved to do his bidding, of the halting little feet that had hastened to his calling.

"Is it thy spirit, O my love?" he wailed. "Is it thy spirit, O dear, dead love?"

A mist came before his eyes, and his heart gave a great cry.

But the fairy dance went on and on. The others swept to and fro and round and round, but the little hunchback danced always on the violets, and through the other music there could be plainly heard, as it crept in and out, the mournful cadence of those tenderer flowers.

And, with the music and the dancing, the night faded into morning. And all at once the music ceased and the little folk could be seen no more. The birds came from their nests, the brook began to bestir himself, and the breath of the new-born day called upon all in that quiet valley to awaken.

So many years have passed since the old poet, sitting under the three lindens half a league the other side of Pesth, saw the fairies dance and heard the fairy music,—so many years have passed since then, that had the old poet not left us an echo of that fairy waltz there would be none now to believe the story I tell.

Who knows but that this very night the elves and the fairies will dance in the quiet valley; that Little Sorrowful will tinkle her maimed feet upon the singing violets, and that the little folk will illustrate in their revels, through which a tone of sadness steals, the comedy and pathos of our lives? Perhaps no one shall see, perhaps no one else ever did see, these fairy people dance their pretty dances; but we who have heard old Robert Volkmann's waltz know full well that he at least saw that strange sight and heard that wondrous music.

And you will know so, too, when you have read this true story and heard old Volkmann's claim to immortality.

Eugene Field – A Short Biography

Eugene Field was born on 2nd September, 1850 in St. Louis, Missouri at 634 S. Broadway to parents Roswell Martin and Frances Reed Field, both of New England stock. Tragically Field lost his mother at age 6 and was thereafter brought up by a cousin, Mary Field French, in Amherst, Massachusetts.

Field attended Williams College in Williamstown, Massachusetts.

When he was 19 his father died, and Field dropped out of Williams. Field's father, Roswell Martin Field, was the lawyer for Dred Scott, the slave who famously sued for his freedom. The complaint was sometimes referred to as 'The lawsuit that started the Civil War'.

Field then went to Knox College in Galesburg, Illinois, but again dropped out. This time after a year. However he did then summon himself to attend the University of Missouri in Columbia, Missouri, where his brother Roswell was studying. As can be gathered from his efforts to date Field was not the most serious of students but was gaining the reputation of being a prankster. Among his more outlandish attempts were a raid on the president's wine cellar, painting the president's house in school colors, and firing the school's landmark cannons at midnight.

Field tried acting but found it not to his liking, studied law but with little success, but did have an interest in writing for the student newspaper.

When his studies finished in 1871, although he never graduated, he collected his share of his inheritance from his father's estate, and set off for a trip to explore Europe. After six months, with funds from the inheritance exhausted, he returned to the United States.

Field then set to work as a journalist for the St. Joseph Gazette in Saint Joseph, Missouri, in 1875.

That same year he married the sixteen-year-old Julia Sutherland Comstock of St Joseph, Missouri. They would eventually have eight children during their twenty-two years of marriage, of whom only five would reach adulthood. Field, knowing that his understanding of finances was somewhat poor, arranged for all the money he earned to be sent to his wife for her to administer on behalf of the family.

In his career as a journalist he soon found a niche that suited him. His articles were light, humorous and written in a personal and gossipy style that endeared him to his readership. Some were soon being syndicated to other newspapers around the States. Field rose to be the city editor of the Gazette.

From 1876 through 1880, the Family lived in St. Louis. Field worked initially as an editorial writer for the Morning Journal and then for the Times-Journal. From there he worked for a short time as the managing editor of the Kansas City Times before settling, for two years, as the editor of the Denver Tribune. He also wrote a column for the paper, 'Odds and Ends,' poking fun at the climate, the muddy roads, the frontier language, and other aspects of Denver life. However his readership was large and growing. Further opportunities would come.

In 1883 the Field moved the family to Chicago lured by a salary of $50 a week. Field now began work for the Chicago Daily News. Here he wrote his humorous newspaper column called Sharps and Flats. He quickly found out that $50 dollars in Denver didn't stretch that far in bustling Chicago.

His column ran in the newspaper's morning edition. In it Field made quips about issues and personalities of the day, especially regarding the arts and literature. His pet subject was the intellectual superiority of Chicago, especially when he compared it to Boston, which he often did. In

April 1887, he wrote, "While Chicago is humping herself in the interests of literature, art and the sciences, vain old Boston is frivoling away her precious time in an attempted renaissance of the cod fisheries."

In another article that year after Chicago's National League baseball club sold future baseball Hall of Famer Mike "King" Kelly to Boston which overlapped with a speaking tour visit from the famous Boston poet and diplomat James Russell Lowell he wrote: "Chicago feels a special interest in Mr. Lowell at this particular time because he is perhaps the foremost representative of the enterprising and opulent community which within the last week has secured the services of one of Chicago's honored sons for the base-ball season of 1887. The fact that Boston has come to Chicago for the captain of her baseball nine has reinvigorated the bonds of affection between the metropolis of the Bay state and the metropolis of the mighty west; the truth of this will appear in the mighty welcome which our public will give Mr. Lowell next Tuesday."

It was in 1888 that his poem 'Little Boy Blue' was printed in America, a weekly journal. It achieved for Field instant and lasting fame. Coincidentally the same issue carried a poem by James Russell Lowell. Field was immensely pleased that his own poem was regarded with considerably more weight and acclaim.

Field had first published poetry in 1879, when his poem 'Christmas Treasures' was published. It later appeared in 'A Little Book of Western Verse' (1889). This was the beginning that would eventually number over a dozen volumes. He developed a style of light-hearted poems for children. Among the perennial favorites are 'Wynken, Blynken, and Nod' and 'The Duel' (but better known as 'The Gingham Dog and the Calico Cat') and 'Little Boy Blue' about the death of a child. As well as verse Field published an extensive range of short stories including 'The Holy Cross' and 'Daniel and the Devil.'

Field treasured rare, unusual and beautiful books and his personal library had scores of them. He also enjoyed making them too and frequently worked long hours with great care and various colored inks decorating the first letter of his poems.

In 1889 whilst the family were in London and Field himself was recovering from a bout of ill health he wrote his most famous poem; 'Lovers Lane'. It is often thought to have been written whilst the couple were courting but recent research settles it authorship to this later date. The poem was written as a reminder of better days when the couple courted in her father's buggy on 'Lover's Lane, St Jo'.

Field was ever curious and keen to push his boundaries. In 1891 with his brother Roswell they wrote and published 'Echoes from the Sabine Farm' a loosely translated version of Horace.

On 4th November 1895 Eugene Field Sr died in Chicago of a heart attack at the age of 45. He is buried at the Church of the Holy Comforter in Kenilworth, Illinois.

The New York Times described his death: CHICAGO, Nov. 4. — Eugene Field, the poet and humorist, died at 5 o'clock this morning of heart disease at his residence in Buena Park. Although Mr. Field had been ill for the past three days, his sudden death was totally unexpected.

Field was originally interred at Graceland Cemetery in Chicago, but his son-in-law, Senior Warden of the Church of the Holy Comforter, had him reinterred on 7th March, 1926.

Several of his poems were set to music with commercial success. Many of his works were accompanied by paintings from the exceptional talents of Maxfield Parrish.

During his lifetime he was often referred to as the 'poet of childhood'. This may account for his anonymous publication of 'Only a Boy'. In our own times the work would probably be frowned upon. It concerns a 12-year-old boy being seduced by a woman in her 30s. The 1920's drama critic/magazine editor George Jean Nathan claimed it was a popular but forbidden work among those coming of age in the early 1900's.

Much of what Field wrote was light, humourous and of its time. And that is perhaps why it has endured. Its writes of a time that, in his words, suspends itself from the harsh reality of real life to a gentler and more touching time that exists in the imagination.

Eugene Field – A Concise Bibliography

The Tribune Primer (1882)
Culture's Garland (1887)
A Little Book of Profitable Tales (1889)
A Little Book of Western Verse (1889)
With Trumpet and Drum (1892)
Echoes from the Sabine Farm (1893)
The Holy Cross and Other Tales (1893)
Second Book of Verse (1893)
Love Songs of Childhood (1894)
Love Affairs of a Bibliomaniac (1895)
Little Willie (1895)
Songs and Other Verse (1896)
Second Book of Tales (1896)
The House; An Episode in the Lives of Reuben Baker, Astronomer and His Wife Alice (1896)
Field Flowers (1896)
Florence Bardsley's Story (1897)
Lullaby Songs of Childhood (1897)
Lullaby Land (1898)
Sharps and Flats (1900)
The Stars (1901)
Nonsense for Old and Young (1901)
A Little Book of Nonsense (1901)
A Little Book of Tribune Verse (1901)
The Sabine Farm (1903)
John Smith USA (1905)
The Clink of Ice (1905)
Hoosier Lyrics (1905)
Cradle Lullabies (1909)
The Poems of Eugene Field (1910)
Christmas Tales and Christmas Verse (1912)
Penn-Yan Bill's Wooing (1914)
The Yankee Abroad (1917)
The Mouse and the Moonbeam (1919)
Poems of Childhood (1920)

The Gingham Dog and the Calico Cat (1926)
Child Verses (1927)
The Sugar Plum Tree (1929)
In Wink-a-way Land (1930)